THE UNSEEN II

BRYAN SMITH

Grindhouse Press
PO BOX 540
Yellow Springs, Ohio 45387

Grindhouse Press #085
ISBN-13: 978-1-941918-99-9

For Roxie

Other titles by Bryan Smith

Rock and Roll Reform School Zombies
Darkened
Highways to Hell
The Dark Ones
Some Crazy Fucking Shit That Happened One Day
The Freakshow
Soultaker
House of Blood
Queen of Blood
Grimm Awakening
Blood and Whiskey
The Halloween Bride
The Diabolical Conspiracy
Deathbringer
Strange Ways
Slowly We Rot
Surrounded By Bastards
The Reborn
Bloodrush
All Hallow's Dead
Christmas Eve on Haunted Hill
Seven Deadly Tales of Terror

ONE

SITTING SLOUCHED DOWN IN A chair in her gloomy, debris-strewn living room, Allison Cook watched a gory scene play out on her big 4K TV. It was mounted on the wall above her vintage floor model Zenith, a relic from the mid-70s she used for watching VHS movies. The film she now watched was on DVD, a slightly more modern format she actually liked less than VHS. Yes, technically, the picture was better than videotape, but without that crisp ultra-clarity of 4K or Blu-ray. DVDs left her cold. They weren't quite modern enough and they didn't push that sweet nostalgia button in the right way.

In this case, she didn't have a choice in the matter. When The Visitor gifted her with movies from other places—from other *worlds*—he didn't present her with an array of format choices from which she could choose. There was nothing convenient or easy about the way it worked. Sometimes he gave her VHS movies recorded from cable. Other times they were ex-rental tapes from alternate reality video stores with unfamiliar names. A few of her special VHS movies looked pristine, as if they were fresh from the factory. Hell, maybe they were. She had the impression her otherworldly benefactor moved around in time in addition to shifting between realities. Much more frequently the movies were on DVD or Blu-ray. A small handful were 4K discs.

The movie playing right now was *Friday the 13th Part X: Reckoning.*

This one was about an elite team of highly trained mercenaries hired to track down and capture Jason Voorhees and finally put an end to his long reign of terror. The mercenaries were mostly cocky ex-soldiers who failed to take their undead adversary as seriously as they should have. There was a definite *Aliens* vibe to that part of it. She doubted this was unintentional. One by one, Jason dispatched the mercenaries in spectacularly gruesome ways until there was just one left, who of course was the squad's only female member. This was as expected. It wasn't a proper slasher movie without a final girl, even if the final girl in this case wasn't quite cut from the usual helpless mode.

Allison liked this installment, which came as a pleasant surprise. The military trappings filled her with misgivings at the outset. She liked her *Friday* movies to follow the usual formula. Partying teens in the woods. Illicit sex in the outdoors. Nudity and substance abuse. Any divergences from this she usually found unwelcome. Her worries were soon put to rest, however, as these elements did eventually come into play.

Reckoning was also the second movie in the franchise to be filmed in 3D. Second that she knew of, anyway. Who knew what else was floating around out there in the goddamn multiverse. The three-dimensional process used in this one was notably superior to that used in 1982's *Friday the 13th Part 3 in 3-D*, but still not nearly as advanced as modern 3D technology. The only bummer was having to watch it at home instead of at a proper theatrical presentation, but in the end, she was just grateful the disc came with the necessary 3D glasses.

She knew from studying the film's credits it was originally released in 1993. In some other reality's version of 1993, anyway. No version of this movie existed in her own reality. As a diehard fan of the franchise, she found much to recommend in it, even if she didn't like it quite as much as *Part IX: Homecoming*. But that movie was a goddamn slasher masterpiece and would've been impossible to top anyway, so she couldn't hold that against it.

The weird thing was *Reckoning* did not seem to follow along the same timeline as *Homecoming*. There were no references to any of the characters or situations from that film, including several things she was certain fans of the franchise probably considered iconic in the reality in which *Homecoming* was released. Even stranger was the way *Reckoning* seemed to reference story elements with which she was wholly unfamiliar. Early in the film a female character identified as the only survivor of the most recent Crystal Lake massacre was killed in her home, an obvious fan service throwback to *Part II*. Jason dunked her face in a pot of boiling water and then used the pot to bludgeon her to death. It was a cool scene, one she figured she would've liked even more if she'd ever seen the previous sequel that featured the character in a starring role.

She could only conclude that *Reckoning* did not come from the same reality as *Homecoming*. It was the only theory that sensibly reconciled these major divergences. Because she loved *Homecoming* so much, she begged The Visitor to bring her the tenth film in the franchise, if such a film existed in any other timeline. The DVD of *Reckoning* was in her hands the following day. Her excitement was off the charts, but it ebbed some when she began to pick up on the things that were off-kilter about it.

Allison sipped from her half-empty can of warm beer and glanced at the chair to her right. "You know what this means, right?" She gestured at the screen with the can. "Somewhere out there, in whatever world this one's from, there's an alternate version of *Part IX*. One with a completely different story from *Homecoming*. I really want to see that one. I've asked him for it I don't know how many fucking times, but all I get is silence. I *know* he can get it. He just doesn't want to let me have it yet. Because, I don't know, I haven't let him drain out my entire fucking soul yet. Or maybe he's just being mean. Toying with me." She sighed heavily and sipped from the can again. "Jesus, listen to me ramble. You're being so quiet over there. What do you think?"

Cassie Wainwright shifted in her uncomfortable chair, making the links in her chain clink. "I don't know."

Allison could feel her face twitching as she struggled to contain the rage brewing inside her. "*I don't know.*" She sneered as she said it, her tone full of mockery. "Jesus. That's your favorite fucking phrase. I bet you've said it a hundred-thousand times. Is there anything you *do* know?"

Cassie sniffled and looked at her with wet eyes. "I . . ."

Allison made a sound of disgust.

She drained the last of the beer, crumpled the can in her fist, and threw it at the other woman. It bounced off the side of Cassie's head and tumbled to the floor, where it joined a handful of other empties on the soiled carpet. Proper housekeeping was no longer one of her top priorities. It'd been that way for six months now, since shortly after she'd killed Mark Castleberry and walked away from his uncle's house in Illinois.

Cassie was openly sobbing now.

Allison stared at her in that same withering way a moment longer.

Then she grabbed the remote control, paused the movie, and got up and walked out of the living room.

TWO

THE LIFE ALLISON HAD TODAY scarcely resembled her former one. It was so drastically different she often had difficulty believing only six months separated her present grim reality from the more or less normal existence she'd led for so long. She'd always been something of a misfit, socially awkward and with only a few close friends. The saving grace of that time was how she'd always felt basically okay about who she was as a person. As a decent human being with a functioning moral compass.

That was no longer the case.

She felt like a stranger in her own skin, some alien creature wearing an Allison Cook mask. The face staring back at her in the bathroom mirror looked haggard and sickly. This was the predictable consequence of months of subsisting on little more than cheap beer and shitty delivery food from Uber Eats.

She remained in front of the mirror a while longer, obsessing over the deterioration in her appearance while listening to Cassie quietly weep in the living room.

The sound of her distress stirred a mild pang of remorse, but this was more like an echo of genuine emotion than the real thing. She wasn't entirely devoid of human feelings, not quite yet, but the psychic energy The Visitor sucked out of her on an irregular basis *had* changed her. She was vastly less empathetic than she once was. News stories about immense human suffering barely moved her at all. Not that she was prone to watching the news much these days. But the thing was, stories like that used to make her cry and feel so bad for the people who were hurting.

Now she just didn't give a shit.

She turned away from the mirror and moved over to the toilet, where she settled herself on the seat to pee for the second time since entering the bathroom. The beer was to blame, of course. She was drinking way too much. That was nothing new, but her intake had increased dramatically just these last couple weeks, a timeframe that roughly corresponded with Cassie's arrival at her home.

Allison wiped, pulled up her panties, and flushed the toilet. The only other item of clothing she had on was a dingy-looking halter top. She'd worn it for several consecutive days. The laundry was another of the many chores she was no longer as conscientious about these days. Since she rarely left the house now, it no longer felt like a big deal to let it slide.

Letting things slide was sort of her thing now.

After washing her hands, she wandered out to the kitchen and snagged two more cans of Natural Light from the fridge. She was on her way back out to the living room when a glimpse of something in her peripheral vision caused her to stop in her tracks and turn toward the overstuffed garbage can.

"Well, shit."

At the top of the overflowing can was a wad of used paper towels. The towels were smeared with the telltale orange tinge of mac and cheese. Nestled in their midst was her phone. How that happened, she did not know. Then again, she did a lot of walking around in a numb, oblivious stupor, feeling disconnected from the world and everything in it. This was hardly the first time she'd found some lost item in a random place.

She retrieved the phone and walked back out to the living room. After dropping the phone on the cluttered coffee table in a careless way, she approached Cassie and stood in front of her, offering one of the cans. She had shackles on her legs, with a brace between them to limit mobility. They were the type used by prisons when transporting high-risk inmates from one facility to another. Her hands, however, were chained in a way allowing more range of motion. She could, for instance, eat something if she wanted.

Or drink a beer, even.

Cassie stared blankly at the can for a moment, her eyes glazing in a way that suggested she wasn't even sure what a can of beer was. This was a false impression, of course, a byproduct of the woman's raw emotional state.

"Take it."

Cassie's bottom lip trembled as she met her gaze. "I . . . don't w-want it."

Allison sighed. "I'm getting tired of your shit. You know that? This is what friends do when they watch movies together. They have some beers. Talk shit about the movie. Laugh and have a good time. But I'm not having a good time with you, Cassie. Not even a little fucking bit. How do you feel about that?"

She lowered her head and said something in a voice so small and weak-sounding it was unintelligible.

Allison sneered. "I'm sorry, I can't fucking hear you. Could you say that again? And please speak up this time, you sniveling wretch."

Cassie sucked in a ragged, wheezy breath and exhaled heavily. Her face was streaked with fresh tears when she raised her head to meet Allison's gaze again. "We're not friends. I don't even know you. Please. *Please*. Stop torturing me. Please let me go."

Allison grunted. "I see."

She set both still-unopened beer cans on the coffee table. Her fingers were wet with condensation from the slowly warming aluminum. She wiped the moisture on Cassie's already wet cheeks.

Then she slapped her.

First with her palm and then with the back of her hand, whipping her head violently from side to side. Cassie yelped from the pain and began sobbing loudly. She normally tried hard to remain quiet while crying because she'd learned that being loudly distressed was a sure way of earning more punishment. This time, however, it seemed she couldn't help it.

Allison grabbed a handful of her hair and twisted it hard in her hand. "Shut up or I'll tear off a piece of your fucking scalp."

Cassie needed a few moments to bring herself under control, but the loud sobbing soon yielded to quieter whimpering and weeping.

Allison nodded. "That's better. Now take it back. You know what I mean."

Cassie sniffled. "I'm sorry. We are friends. I was just being a bitch when I said we weren't."

"And what have I said about being a bitch to your best friend?"

Cassie wiped snot from her nose with the back of a hand, making those chain links clink again. "That it's a personality flaw and I should try harder to work on it and be better."

Allison smiled. "That's right. I'm proud of you for having the courage to admit it. Now are you ready to have that beer and talk about the movie?"

More pitiful sniffling.

Then Cassie wiped her eyes, heaved a big breath, and said, "I'd love that."

Allison gave her one of the beers and took the other one for herself as she again settled into her own chair.

After popping the tab on her beer, she reached for the remote and got the movie rolling again.

THREE

THEY WATCHED THE REST OF *Reckoning*, had another couple beers, and enjoyed some moderately stimulating conversation about the movie. Cassie even contributed a few insights that helped Allison look at aspects of the film in a new and interesting light. Overall, it was her best effort yet at replicating the sort of interactions Allison used to regularly have with her dead friend, the original model Cassie. The one who blew her brains out right in front of her six long months ago. Fear of getting smacked around again was evidently a solid motivating factor.

After watching the credits roll—something she always did to the very end with any movie, regardless of whether she liked it—Allison retrieved the DVD from the player and put it back in its case along with the 3D glasses. She shelved it with the rest of her *Friday the 13th* DVDs. She had full collections of the franchise in every available format—VHS, DVD, Blu-ray, etc. She even had several of the earlier franchise entries on laserdisc.

From the bookcase that housed most of her VHS collection, she selected the *Homecoming* tape and set it on the Zenith next to her top-loading VCR. As she did this, she heard a quiet sound of frustration. A groan Cassie had tried and failed to fully suppress.

Allison again took up a position in front of the bound woman's chair. "Problem?"

Cassie gave her head a rapid, startled shake. "No! No, of course not. It's just that . . ."

She trailed off, apparently afraid to finish her thought.

Allison sneeringly shook her head. "Just spit it out for fuck's sake."

Cassie trembled and wiped more tears from her face. "It's just that we've already watched that one today. Right before *Reckoning*. We watched it twice yesterday and three times the day before that."

Allison nodded contemplatively as the other woman spoke.

Then she said, "And?"

Cassie swallowed with obvious difficulty and forced herself to again meet Allison's steely gaze. "It's just a little much. One movie so many times in a short span. There must be other movies you'd like to watch. Just for a break."

Allison stared at her in absolute silence for a period of minutes.

Cassie made a mewling sound and finally averted her gaze. "I'm sorry. I'm so sorry. I'm just being selfish again. Thinking only of what I want. I swear I'll be better."

Allison nodded. "You sit here for a bit and think about how you can improve your behavior. I'll be in my bedroom, but will be back shortly. By now I shouldn't have to remind you how important it is that you sit quietly and behave. If I hear anything that makes me think you're being bad or doing anything you shouldn't, I'll be out here in a flash."

Cassie sobbed. "Please . . . please don't hurt me again."

"Be good and I won't have to."

Allison grabbed another can of Natural Light and went to her bedroom, leaving the door open a crack. An old VHS camcorder sat at the edge of her dresser opposite the foot of her bed. She pressed the power button on the side of the camera and then the record button. Then she took a seat at the edge of her bed and popped open the beer can.

Summoning the brightest smile she could manage, she looked at the lens of the camera and started talking. "Hi there! It's me again, Allison, everybody's favorite *Friday the 13th* fanatic. So, yeah, this is the part of the movie where you're starting to feel completely mindfucked by the visionary auteur directing the goddamn thing. Like, I can just see you guys sitting at home, watching and going, 'Hey, wasn't that bitch dead as fuck in the last reel? She stuck a gun in her mouth and blew the back of her head open.' So what the fuck, right?"

She stopped talking for a brief time, turning her head to the left to look out her large bedroom window. When the blinds were open, the window afforded her a nice view of her backyard. Well, once upon a time it'd been a nice view. It hadn't been pleasant to gaze upon lately, proper upkeep of the lawn being yet another thing she'd let slide since last summer. Now, though, there was a fresh blanket of snow on the ground, which hid the most telling signs of neglect.

She gulped beer and looked at the camera lens again. "Where was I? Oh, yeah." She manufactured a giggle, a sound meant to signal amusement at her absentmindedness. There was a distinct and unmistakable fake quality to the sound. Whatever. It was a work in progress. "So, here's the thing, guys. That really *is* Cassie Wainwright out there in the living room. Like, for real. She's not some impostor. That isn't deep fake trickery when you see her on camera. That bitch is Cassie, one-hundred percent." A pause for another gulp of beer. "But she's also *not* Cassie. Yeah, I know. Confusing as shit, right?" She sighed. "Okay, so this is going to take some explaining . . ."

FOUR

THE SUDDEN LOSS OF ALLISON'S only real friends left her lonely and miserable. She spent nearly the entire intervening six months alone in her home, never having contact with other humans. Even when she had things delivered, they were left on the porch for her to retrieve after the delivery person was gone. She still had a job with the same company she'd worked at for years, but shortly after the deaths of her friends she requested a transfer to a work-at-home position. The request was granted almost immediately.

There were a couple of different ways of interpreting that. The generous one was that management was showing an unusual level of sensitivity in light of the trauma she'd endured. Her direct supervisor suggested as much at the time. While Allison would like to have taken those words of kindness at face value, her cynical nature wouldn't let her. Management didn't like her. She knew this for a fact, having eavesdropped on too many whispered remarks she wasn't meant to hear. Her coworkers were never overtly hostile toward her, but they weren't friendly either. As in nearly every other social circumstance, she was too weird to fit in with regular people, only able to interact with them in the most stilted of ways. Allowing her to work at home was an easy and painless way of getting her out of the building.

The new position came with reduced hours and pay. Another person might have balked at the income reduction, but Allison was okay with it, at least in the short term. She still had a good chunk of money in her savings account and even at her new lower income level would remain comfortable for at least the next year. Plus the shorter hours meant she'd have so much more time to devote to enjoying The Visitor's gifts.

The way the summoning part of it worked took some figuring out, enough to make her wish she'd spent more time grilling Mark Castleberry about the process before killing him. It was what needed doing, she knew that. She could imagine no scenario in which she would've been comfortable moving forward in a relationship with that guy. He was too broken. Even more broken than her, which was really saying something.

Still, perhaps she could've waited just a bit longer before doing the deed. Long enough to glean a bit more information and guidance. Then again, there would've been risks in doing that as well. He was a damaged creep, but he wasn't stupid. Too many questions might've put him on guard, made him wonder about her motives.

Whatever.

She eventually got the hang of communicating with the interdimensional being. This didn't involve conversing in any normal way, as the creature never actually spoke. She was the only one who did any talking. It was more like a presence she felt in her head, alien thoughts that arrived from outside her consciousness in response to her queries. After some trial and error, she found that by focusing her thoughts while staring at a bottom corner of the bathroom mirror she was able to open a psychic channel in the ether. The opening of the channel was accompanied by a soft popping sound in her ear canal and a strange, disconcerting twitch inside her head.

That first time she felt goosebumps on her arms and knew he was right behind her, standing just inside the bathroom's open door. That moment was a complete game-changer. No longer would she be entirely reliant on waiting for him to randomly materialize. She knew if she shifted her gaze from the corner of the mirror to somewhere in the middle, she would see him standing behind her in his long coat and wide-brimmed hat tipped low over his blurry face.

She kept her gaze right where it was, trembling as she swallowed hard and found the nerve to quietly utter her desire. "I want something. I *need* something. Anything to make me feel happy for just a little while. One of your gifts."

The Visitor reached inside her head, requesting specification.

So she told him what she wanted.

13

Another official *Friday the 13th* film that didn't exist in this reality.

"If one exists," she hastily added, not wishing to seem overly demanding. "I mean, that's definitely my preference, but if you can't get one, I guess I wouldn't mind some alternate *Texas Chainsaw* or *Halloween* sequel instead."

She fell silent then, waiting to see what would happen.

The Visitor did not enter her mind again.

Not that time.

The chill in the bathroom faded and the goosebumps on her arms disappeared.

The Visitor was gone.

When she got up the next day, she went out to her living room to login for work on her laptop. Cassie was slumped in her chair and either asleep or ignoring her. Allison entered her system password, but before hitting the enter key something made her glance toward the Zenith, where she saw a small stack of movies next to her VCR. Two VHS tapes and what looked like a Blu-ray disc. They hadn't been there when she went to bed the previous evening. She shot up from the couch and hurried over to the Zenith to examine the items.

She gasped in delight when she saw the slipcase cover image for the VHS tape at the top of the stack. Then she cackled. The movie was *Chop Top: Texas Chainsaw Massacre IV*. Only a true *Chainsaw* devotee could understand why this was instantly hilarious without knowing anything else about the mysterious movie.

Chop Top was a character introduced in *The Texas Chainsaw Massacre Part 2* in 1986. The next film in the franchise didn't come out until 1990 and was called *Leatherface: Texas Chainsaw Massacre III*. That one completely ignored the events of *Part 2*, creating a new timeline in which Chop Top didn't even exist. Yet here he was again, back in a movie no one in her world had ever seen. The cover image showed Chop Top holding a bloody hammer and leering in his uniquely demented way. Leatherface was lurking in the lurid background with his chainsaw as usual, but the focus here was clearly Chop Top. This pleased Allison immensely. She couldn't wait to watch it.

The second VHS tape didn't have a slipcase. It was another movie on a recordable tape. The label on the side was inked with yet another title she didn't recognize—*Halloween 8: Waking the Dead*. The title made her frown. It was so inscrutable. Without a slipcase description, she couldn't deduce the basics of the plot. Was Michael Myers tangling with zombies in this one or did the word dead refer to ghosts?

Only way to find out was to watch it.

Her heart sank when she saw the Blu-ray at the bottom of the stack. Instead of finding another *Friday the 13th* there—as she fully expected by then, with good reason—what she saw was something called *The Doomed Ones*. She'd never heard of it and it didn't belong to any existing franchise she knew of. Its inclusion with this group of films mystified her. The title was in a gothic font and showed three ghostly looking young women against a stark black background. She screeched in frustration and smacked the disc case against the top of the VCR.

Then a fit of rage overtook her.

She screamed. Multiple times, her lungs turning raw from it. She stomped out of the living room and into the kitchen, where she shoved the Blu-ray deep inside the already full trash can. Her arm sank elbow deep into a mass of dirty napkins, food containers, used coffee filters, crumpled beer cans, and who knew what else. She opened her fingers and let go of the Blu-ray case while her arm was still deep in the trash, leaving it there when she withdrew her arm. Her flesh was slathered in unidentifiable slimy stuff and bits of partly eaten food. She screeched again as she staggered over to the sink to wash off, the contortions of her face reflecting the rage she couldn't control.

Breathing heavily, she shut the tap off, backed away from the sink, and turned her face up toward the ceiling. She screamed again and raged at the top of her voice, accusing The Visitor of intentionally fucking with her. He'd clearly refused to provide her with exactly what she requested out of some form of petty spite. It wasn't until several minutes later, after she was finally able to pull back from the brink of a total mental breakdown, that she began to see things differently.

She felt a deep level of embarrassment for her outburst. She was an adult. A grown-up woman of thirty who'd never been prone to bursts of psychotic rage. She'd been through a lot, yes, but that was no excuse for behaving like a maniac. The calmer she got, the more it scared her how apocalyptically angry she'd gotten. All because of a theoretical movie she'd asked for that maybe didn't even exist anywhere in the multiverse. Maybe *Homecoming* really was the only alternate *Friday the 13th* out there. The Visitor fulfilled her other requests. Thinking he was deliberately fucking with her for some unknown diabolical reason was one hell of an overreaction.

Her eyes filled with tears.

She looked at the ceiling again.

What's wrong with me? Oh, God, what the hell is wrong with me?

She shivered and looked at the trash can again, a sick feeling twisting at her stomach. Alarming memories of her recent past came flooding back, including things Mark had told her about The Visitor's gifts. If sharing them with other people—especially strangers—was dangerous, discarding them was at least as ill-advised. Say she never retrieved that disc from the garbage. Eventually she'd take the bag to the garbage bin outside and shortly thereafter it'd wind up in the back of a waste disposal truck. Then from there to a landfill. She'd never get it back if that happened. Maybe losing it would only truly be dangerous if some desperate scavenger retrieved it at the landfill, but how likely was that?

She frowned.

Fuck.

She went to the garbage can and shoved her arm deep inside the trash again, her hand grasping around for the disc. As she did this, she realized that some of the icky slimy stuff she felt on her skin was vomit from the night before. She groaned in disgust, but kept groping around until her fingers finally closed around the Blu-ray case.

Removing it, she went back to the sink and washed off again. After that, she carefully cleaned off the disc case with a damp paper towel. Then she carried the disc back out to the living room, where she shelved it with the rest of her horror Blu-rays, figuring maybe she'd take a more thorough look at it later, possibly even watch it at some point. For the time being, however, *The Doomed Ones*, whatever it was, wasn't anything she cared about.

She now knew Cassie was feigning sleep. There was no way her outburst wouldn't have woke her.

She popped the *Chainsaw* tape in her VCR, turned on the Zenith, and returned to her couch to settle in and watch the movie. Before hitting the play button on the remote, she glimpsed the black screen of her laptop and abruptly recalled she was supposed to have been logged in for work by now. She swiped at the touchpad and brought the laptop out of sleep mode, grimacing when she saw the time in the bottom right-hand corner of the screen. 8:21 in the morning. Her designated login time was 8:00.

Goddammit.

She considered the situation for only a brief moment before

coming to an impulsive decision. Her phone was on the coffee table next to the laptop. She picked it up and swiped at the screen. No angry messages from her supervisor yet. She preemptively sent a text of her own before that could happen. She was too sick to work. Even just the prospect of sitting at her laptop all day was too exhausting. She apologized and swore she'd be back at it tomorrow. A terse reply came back almost immediately: "OK."

She had to laugh.

They didn't care.

All her virtual absence meant to anyone at the company was less money they'd have to pay her.

She closed her laptop and started the movie.

FIVE

ALLISON EXHALED HEAVILY AND TOOK another gulp of Natural Light. The can she'd brought to the bedroom with her was almost empty. She shook it, frowning as she listened to the meager remaining contents swish around the bottom.

She forced another of those fake sunny smiles and looked at the camcorder. "Gonna need another beer soon, so I guess I better get through the rest of this faster. My special guest is probably wondering what's taking me so long."

On impulse, she killed the rest of the beer, crumpled the can, and dropped it on the floor. There were a few other empties at her feet, left there at the end of other recording sessions.

There was a different quality to her smile when she again brought her gaze back to the lens, a hint of playful naughtiness. "You guys wanna see something I've kept under wraps since last summer?"

She lifted up her top, briefly flashing the camera.

A humorless giggle ensued, followed by a deep sigh. "No one's fucked me since I killed Mark Castleberry. It's so sad. Even a pitiful wretch like me still needs to get some sometimes. Sometimes I think I fucked up by killing that idiot. Whatever else you can say about him, I turned the boy on. He was hot for me and he wasn't the worst fuck I ever had. I could still be getting that every night." Another sigh, more wistful this time. "But, no, I did the right thing. And what's done is done."

She fell silent then and stared at the camera lens for several minutes without speaking. The look on her face was blank, slack, her mouth hanging open and her eyes glazing like someone under the effects of heavy dope. She didn't need to see her face to know she looked that way. She'd seen the expression many times now in her bathroom mirror.

The corners of her mouth slowly began to tip upward in a dazedly amused expression. "Sorry, spaced out again. I've been doing that a lot lately. Probably has to do with drinking so goddamn much. Anyway, getting that first batch of movies I asked for marked the true beginning of my downward spiral. I watched them over and over, just like I did with *Homecoming*. Obsessively. It was still a rush to see things no one else in this world ever had. I fucking *reveled* in it. And now that I had some idea of how to summon The Visitor, I started doing it a lot more. He brought me so many fucking treasures. Mostly movies, obviously. Because when you get down to it, what else really matters? Movies are everything. Movies are *life*. But I have gotten a few other cool things. Couple Stephen King books that don't exist here. A Nirvana album from 1997, because apparently there's some other plane of existence where Kurt didn't choke on a shotgun."

She frowned. "Now I'm gonna tell you about the problem I ran into with all that. Well, okay, there were lots of problems. My obsession with the gifts became so all-consuming the rest of my life fell apart. Like, no shit, right? I'm a mess and I know it. So don't be fooled by how fucking glamorous I look on camera." The ensuing giggle felt like the phoniest one yet. "But the big problem, the one that led to my current fucked up beyond all recognition situation, was my loneliness." She shook her head, rolling her eyes. "Fucking ridiculous, I know. I've always been your basic loner, but I did have a couple good friends before all this terribleness started. People I loved who I could talk to about the things I cared about. We'd even hang out and have fun sometimes. But all that went away when Cassie and Julia died."

Allison stood up and gnawed on a thumbnail as she did a bit of impulsive, nervous pacing about in her room. She kicked aside some of the empty beer cans with one of her bare feet and muttered curses. Images of her dead friends assailed her, a form of mental torture she could never quite get drunk enough to push away forever. The spray of Cassie's blood and brains. The way she dropped dead to the fucking floor, falling so near Julia's bullet-riddled body. No spark of life left in either of them. They were just pretty bags of dead meat on a bloody floor.

She sat again as abruptly as she'd stood and again addressed the camera. "I went to some really dark places in my head, guys. I thought about killing myself a lot. Like, all day every day for weeks on end. I'd sit there drunk on my couch and just picture it. The barrel of a gun in my mouth. My finger on the cold trigger. The loud bang and the spray of red behind me. There was a fucked-up appeal to going out just like Cassie." She shrugged. "Obviously I didn't do that. Didn't have the guts, if you want to know the truth. But still I was unbearably lonely. I started pretending other people were in the room with me when I watched my special movies, had whole pretend conversations. It was a special new level of ultra-pathetic. So it was probably inevitable that I'd start to wonder if The Visitor could bring me things other than mere objects. I'll just go ahead and say it. A few weeks ago I asked him to bring me another Cassie. I figured if there are infinite alternate realities, then in some of them there must be other versions of my dead friends. At first I thought he wouldn't do it. Days went by. I tried summoning him again. He wouldn't come. But then—"

A sound from somewhere outside her room caused Allison's head to snap toward her cracked-open door.

She listened a moment longer before groaning in annoyance and bringing her gaze back to the camera. "Sorry, guys. Gonna have to cut this one short. I hear someone misbehaving. We'll save the rest of this for another time, okay?" She waved at the camera. "Bye now."

She went to the camera and stopped the recording.

Then, with her face set in a grimly furious expression, she yanked her door open and stalked out to the living room.

SIX

"WHERE DO YOU THINK YOU'RE GOING?"

Cassie was at the front door. She had her hand on the doorknob and was twisting at it, making the chain links rattle. The chair was on the floor right behind her in the foyer. Because the chains attached to her wrist shackles were wound so loosely through the slats that comprised the chair back, she'd been able to pick it up and carry it with her. Even if she'd been able to open the door, she wouldn't have been able to get very far like that. Far too awkward and cumbersome. Her plan was probably just to get outside and start screaming for help. Might even have worked if she'd had the key to unlock the deadbolt.

Cassie yelped in fright.

Instead of immediately giving up the doomed escape attempt, Cassie jerked at the doorknob harder and harder. To no avail, of course. Allison grabbed hold of the length of chain looped around her waist and yanked her backward, making her gasp again as she flopped back into the chair. She tipped the chair backward, took a firm grip on the top slat, and dragged the chair and guest out of the foyer and back into the living room, parking the chair in the same spot as before.

She put her hands on Cassie's shoulders and bore down hard, leaning over her from behind. "That was dumb. Did you think you were going to rip the door off its hinges?"

Cassie whimpered and muttered something unintelligible.

"What was that? I didn't quite hear you." Allison bore down harder, her hands sliding ever so slightly toward Cassie's neck. "Could you say it again, please?"

Cassie raised her voice. "I don't know what I thought. I'm fucking desperate. I just want out of here so bad."

Allison was silent a moment as she continued to exert pressure on Cassie's shoulders.

Then she said, "Well, that was rude."

She wrapped her hands around Cassie's neck and began to squeeze. At first it was just enough pressure to cause discomfort, but then she tightened her grip, making her gag. As the pressure continued to increase, she tried twisting away from the choking hands, but Allison only bore down harder.

"Stay still while I punish you or I'll choke you to death. I'm not kidding."

Cassie squealed in terror, but she complied as soon as she understood Allison's threat wasn't an empty one.

Allison maintained the pressure on Cassie's throat a while longer just to drive the point home, keeping her grip tight enough to hurt without actually suffocating her.

Then she took her hands away from Cassie's neck.

Cassie sucked in a wheezing breath and started crying again.

Allison swatted the back of her head. "Stop that."

Cassie did her best to bring her loud weeping under control, but continued to mewl softly.

Good enough, Allison decided.

She went into the kitchen and grabbed two more cans of Natural Light from the dwindling case in the fridge. Peering into the carton to assess the situation, she concluded she'd have to obtain more beer before the end of the day. There wasn't enough left to get her through the night. Plus if she didn't replenish her supply now she wouldn't be able to have her morning wake-up beer, a thing too horrible to contemplate.

Back in the living room, she offered one of the cans to Cassie. The woman glanced at it warily, but hesitated only a brief moment before accepting it, apparently in no hurry to receive another violent rebuke.

Allison used the Drizly app on her phone to order two more cases of Natural Light. Even at her current greatly accelerated rate of consumption, forty-eight fresh cans in addition to what she still had should last her a bit. Two or three days, maybe.

She set her phone down and opened her own can.

She took a big gulp and glanced at Cassie. "I've got some more beer on the way. I'm thinking maybe we wait to start the movie until after it gets here. That okay with you?"

Cassie looked perplexed, as if she couldn't understand why she was even being asked. "Um . . . okay? I mean . . . sure, that's fine with me."

Allison smirked. "You look so confused. I was just being polite by pretending to care what you think. The thing is, I don't like being interrupted when I'm watching a movie. Makes me want to tear out a motherfucker's eyeballs."

She laughed and gulped beer.

Cassie sipped from her own can and stared bleakly at the floor.

A period of near total silence ensued. The women sat there and drank their beers without saying a word for more than ten minutes. The only sounds other than their own breathing were the humming of the fridge from the kitchen and the heat coming on.

The silence ended when Cassie cleared her throat and found the nerve to speak. "Can I ask you something?"

Allison looked up from her phone.

She'd been immersed in scrolling through her social feeds, vicariously experiencing the digital lives of her casual acquaintances, most of whom she knew from various corners of online horror fandom. None were close friends, but it was her one way of remaining at least tenuously connected to her former life. Many of them were just returning from another horror convention, this one in Texas. They were sharing con photos and stories. It filled her with a bitter nostalgia for the days when she'd semi-regularly attend such events with Cassie and Julia.

It was starting to get to her and she was grateful for the sudden distraction. She sipped some beer and said, "Okay. Ask me something."

Cassie's eyes were shiny with unshed tears as she met Allison's gaze, but this time she didn't flinch or look away. "You said you brought me here to replace your dead friend. Because you were lonely. You wanted to fill a hole in your life."

Allison nodded. "That's right. We've been through this, though. Many times. I'm not making any of it up, no matter how crazy it sounds. Do I need to show you the pictures again? The videos?

You're exact replicas of each other, down to your names and background. Okay, a few minor details are different, but all the major stuff is the same. You're her and she was you. Sort of."

Cassie sighed. "Yes, the evidence is overwhelming. I believe you. There's one big difference we both know about, but basically you're right. Still, that's not what I want to know."

"Then what is?"

Cassie seemed more hesitant now, more outwardly fearful, but determined to press on anyway. "If your motivation in bringing me here truly was only to have a friend again, then why do you like hurting me so much?"

"I don't—"

"You do!" Cassie snapped back, clearly not interested in hearing a denial. "I don't know why you're even bothering to pretend otherwise. You get off on hurting me. You *enjoy* it. If you want the truth, I think your original reason for bringing me here doesn't even matter anymore. I think the pleasure you get from torturing me has surpassed everything else."

Allison's mouth slowly curled into an angry sneer. "Hmm. Interesting. You want to know what *I* think?"

Cassie's resoluteness of purpose disintegrated immediately upon hearing the hard tone of her captor. Her face crumpled as tears began gushing from her red-rimmed eyes again.

"Please . . ."

"Shut up."

Cassie moaned in distress but said nothing further.

Allison's sneer became a smile. "I think you need to go back down to the basement, spend the rest of the day in your filthy fucking crate. In the dark, alone with your stupid fucking thoughts for hours on end."

Cassie's mouth fell open as she began to wail at an ear-piercingly shrill level.

Allison got up and slapped her repeatedly until the wailing subsided.

Then she grabbed hold of the chair and dragged Cassie out of the living room.

SEVEN

GETTING CASSIE PROPERLY SECURED IN the basement took longer than usual. She struggled with raw-edged desperation, squirming and screaming the whole time. Grappling with her was more a source of aggravation than anything else. She wasn't getting loose. The shackles and leg brace would see to that.

Allison was eventually able to wrestle her into the crate, but at one point she took an elbow to the chin. This pissed her off so much she left the leg brace on instead of removing it, as she normally did when it was time to confine Cassie to the crate. Served her right. Now the bitch wouldn't be able to get comfortable amidst the mass of dirty old blankets. Cassie raised up and spat at her as Allison clapped the padlock in place and locked it.

Allison wiped spittle from her face and smiled. "It's like you're asking for it at this point. This is on you. Remember that."

She went upstairs and grabbed a broom from the hallway closet, taking it back down to the basement with her. Cassie backed herself into a rear corner of the crate and started pleading as soon as she saw it. Allison laughed and started jabbing at her through the slats of the crate with the blunt end of the handle. Her guest absorbed hard blows to her abdomen, back, neck, and face as she continually tried twisting away from it. One blow gouged one of her eyes pretty severely. Allison laughed again and kept on jabbing at her.

This went on for several minutes.

Then Allison abruptly broke off the assault and said, "Remember what I told you. This is on you. You could be upstairs enjoying a movie with me right now, getting drunk and having a good time, just like we used to before you killed yourself, you stupid cunt. Instead you get to spend the rest of your day in this piss-stinking crate. Use this time to think about how you can be better when I let you out tomorrow."

She headed for the unvarnished wooden staircase leading back upstairs. Cassie resumed pleading as she began to climb the steps. She swore she'd be better, saying she'd finally learned her lesson. Allison smiled and said nothing. She flicked off the light as she reached the top step. Then she stepped out into the hallway and closed and locked the door behind her.

After returning the broom to the hallway closet, she went into her bedroom and stashed the basement key in the top drawer of her nightstand. She glanced at the dark lens of the camcorder and considered resuming her interrupted recording session. With Cassie put away until tomorrow, she could take her time about getting back to watching movies. She could do a longer than usual session, get some of her more complicated thoughts about her situation on tape with no worries about being interrupted again.

She shrugged.

Okay, sure, why not?

Instead of immediately starting the recording again, however, she decided to fetch some more beers from the kitchen. On impulse, she veered away from the kitchen once she reached the end of the hallway. She went into the living room and then into the foyer, where she peeked through a window and saw a young man in jeans and a Blue Jackets hoodie walking up the sidewalk toward her porch. Obviously the Drizly delivery person, an easy deduction based on the cases of Natural Light he was carrying.

Oh, shit.

She ran back to her bedroom, where her purse was on the nightstand. She fished out her wallet and keys and went running back down the hallway again. Her heart was pounding by the time she reached the front door, at which point the delivery guy was climbing the steps to the porch.

She'd almost forgotten.

Food and grocery deliveries could be left on the porch for her to retrieve at her convenience.

Alcohol deliveries, on the other hand, required an ID check.

She unlocked the door and pulled it open.

The delivery guy started to say something, but the unexpected sight of her in her underwear appeared to temporarily short circuit his brain. His mouth moved a few times, but no words emerged.

Allison smiled.

She stepped out onto the little porch with him, crowding him backward as she pulled the door into the frame behind her without fully shutting it. The cold air made her shiver, but she didn't care. The delivery guy was young, early twenties at the most. He was also more than acceptably cute. Nothing close to movie-star handsome, but pleasant enough to look at.

She looked him up and down and said, "Do you want to fuck me?"

The short circuiting of his brain became more pronounced. His face twitched and he started blinking rapidly.

Allison reached behind her, touched the doorknob. "Come on. We can do it in the foyer. You can have me fast against the wall. Then you can be on your way to your next stop with hardly any delay." She laughed again, in what she hoped was a seductive way. "It'll be like a hot porn clip, something you can carry in your spank bank forever. A wild story you can tell your friends. The only thing is, I'll need you to keep it quiet while we're inside. No moaning or anything. I'd say why, but it's complicated."

The delivery guy swallowed hard and found his voice at last. "Um . . . I don't think so."

Allison frowned. "Why not?"

He grimaced. "Well . . . for one thing, you reek. It's like you took a bath in a tub of stale beer. And you sort of look like you haven't showered in weeks. I'm sorry, I'm not trying to be an asshole. Just telling it like it is. This doesn't feel like a good situation."

Allison's expression turned sullen.

She flipped open her wallet, took out her ID, and handed it over.

The delivery guy scanned the back of it with his phone and gave it back. Leaving the cases of beer at the edge of the porch, he started to turn away from her, but she seized him by the crook of an arm.

"I could pay you."

He stood frozen there a moment before turning slowly toward her again, a disbelieving look on his face. "What?"

She felt embarrassed for herself even in the midst of making this proposition. This was a new low, even for her. This was the previously unknown bottom that existed beyond so-called rock bottom. This moment of shameful self-awareness did not, however, stop her from pressing on.

"Do you have Venmo? I could send you a hundred dollars right now." She smirked. "I'm guessing you're not rolling in cash, otherwise you wouldn't be doing this delivery bullshit. A hundred dollars for two minutes' work. You really turning that down?"

He didn't respond right away, but she could tell he was seriously considering it.

She slipped a finger inside one of his belt loops and tugged him a little closer. Out in the street, a horn honked as a car drove by, probably in appreciation of her underdressed state.

"Wear a condom if you're so worried about fucking a dirty drunk bitch."

She tugged him even closer and he allowed it.

Then he placed his hands on her shoulders, putting a firm stop to it. "I just can't. This feels really fucking wrong somehow."

He backed away from her and hopped off the porch, hitting the ground running as he sprinted toward a red Mazda parked at the curb. Allison felt bitter anger rise up inside her as she watched him go. She stayed where she was as he started his car, pulled away from the curb, and sped off.

"Fuck you," she said to the empty yard in front of her.

She huffed out a despondent breath, grabbed the cases of beer, and went back inside.

EIGHT

ALLISON CARRIED THE CASES OF beer into the kitchen and set them on the dining table. Once they were out of her hands, she spent time raging, screaming and kicking at one of the chairs arrayed around the table. She picked it up and slammed it against the edge of the counter, splintering one of the legs. The chair bounced out of her grip and went skidding across the floor. She picked it up and smashed it against the edge of the counter multiple more times, until the broken leg came off completely.

With this act of destruction completed, she stood there breathing heavily for several moments as the rage drained out of her. She stared at the shattered remnants of the chair and wondered—not for the first time—what was wrong with her. She was losing more of her mind every day. But she didn't ponder this question for long because she knew *exactly* what was happening to her and why. She just felt powerless to stop it or even slow it down.

She unlocked the French doors that opened onto her small back deck and carried the broken remnants of the chair outside. Her bare feet crunched on the layer of snow covering the deck as she hurled the broken pieces of the chair into her backyard. Not the ideal disposal method for a ruined piece of furniture, but she was too drunk and pissed off to give a shit. More snow was on the way, so the pieces would get covered up for a while anyway.

She went back inside and stamped her feet on the rug just inside the door, grumbling to herself about hypothermia. It was all too easy to imagine herself storming outside like this while completely blasted and passing out in the snow. If that ever happened, she was fucked. There was no one around to look after her or check in on her. Well . . . no one she could trust, anyway.

After belatedly stowing the new cases of Natural Light in the fridge, she took two more cans from the already open carton and carried them with her to her bedroom. She smiled as she moved past the door to the basement, thinking about Cassie crying down there in the dark. Thinking about how scared she must be, being so impossibly far from home, beyond the reach of anyone who cared about her. Beyond help of any kind. Allison didn't feel sorry for her. Things could be so different if the bitch ever made any genuine effort to bond with her. She was so fucking selfish.

Back in the bedroom now, she turned on the camcorder and hit the record button. She situated herself at her normal spot on the edge of the bed, opening one of the beers after setting the extra can on the floor.

She again summoned one of her fake sunny smiles and said, "Hey, guys. Back a little sooner than I expected. Sorry to bail on you so abruptly earlier, but my troublesome guest was being bad again. I thought we'd spend the rest of the day watching movies, but she kept on being an obnoxious fucking brat, so I had to put her away for the night." She took a sip of beer and sighed. "Honestly, I don't know how much longer I can do this. She's wearing me out with her incessant misbehavior. With some people you just reach a point where you have to say, 'Enough is enough.' You know?"

She gulped beer and said nothing for almost a full minute. Her fake smile vanished as her face took on a contemplative cast. She gnawed on her bottom lip and glanced at the window, again slipping into the nervous habit that plagued her during these recording sessions.

There was no one watching her as she made these recordings. The camera itself wasn't sentient. It was just a machine. A primitive one with no connection to the internet. A machine incapable of passing judgment or making her feel small with a smirk or withering remark. It was unlikely anyone else would ever see these tapes. Not until after she was dead, at least. So there was no logical reason she should be nervous while recording. Not that she was allowing logic to factor into her thinking often these days. The nervousness was there anyway, whether it made sense or not, and she felt powerless to change that.

Allison brought her gaze back to the camera lens, not bothering to force a smile this time. "Anyway, by now I guess it's pretty obvious I have some unresolved anger issues where Cassie is concerned. We were friends, yes. Great friends. I fucking loved her. But she was mean to me before she died. Cruel, even." Tears welled in her eyes and she tried blinking them back, but a single bead of moisture rolled slowly down her cheek. "I mean, yeah, it wasn't *all* her fault. The *Homecoming* tape was influencing her. Same as it did to Julia. It got inside their heads and fucked with their thinking. Cassie wasn't in her right mind when she said those awful things to me. And yet . . ." Another quick glance at the window followed by a deep slug of beer. She looked at the camera. "I think those mean thoughts were already in her head, somewhere deep inside. Buried. The tape just brought it all to the surface."

She leaned back a little, bracing one hand on the mattress. "It made me feel like what we had was never real in the first place. But then I think about all the good times, and all the times she was there for me when I was feeling low. She made me feel like I mattered. I almost never felt that way before she and Julia came into my life. They made me feel like I wasn't just a lonely loser. Like I had a place in this world. I just wish I could get *that* version of Cassie back. Is that so much to ask?"

A big yawn surprised her.

She flopped backward onto the mattress and stared at the ceiling, the half-empty can of Natural Light still grasped loosely in her fingers. "I keep asking the same questions over and over, I know. I just can't seem to find any answers. Not any I like, anyway."

Her eyelids began to droop and she felt herself drifting toward unconsciousness. She found it an enticing prospect. Sleep would be nice. A few solid hours of oblivion might be just what she needed to clear the cobwebs from her head and start seeing things more clearly. She continued to drift until she felt the slick beer can start to slide free of her loosening fingers.

She tightened her grip on the can and sat woozily upright again, laughing as she looked at the camera. "Fuck. Maybe I should get up and put on a pot of coffee. It's not even dark out yet. Way too early to be passing out."

She laughed again.

Then her traitorous mind abruptly veered back to the embarrassing encounter with the delivery guy. She wished she could drive it from her mind, cut it out with a knife maybe, but she knew that wasn't possible. It was going to be one of those things that intermittently came back to taunt her for the rest of her life. She'd been on the verge of paying a random man for sex. It'd been a sincere proposition. There was no doubt she would've gone through with it if he'd been game. Now, however, the thought made her stomach churn with disgust.

Did she have no self-respect remaining?

Apparently not.

Her expression hardened as she sneered at the camera. "Men are garbage. I've yet to meet even one worth a damn." She downed the rest of the beer and hurled the can across the room. "My heterosexuality is a fucking curse. I hate it. I hate everything about me."

She got up and wobbled over to the dresser, where she stopped the recording before grabbing the other can of beer. The can fizzed as she popped it open and stumbled out of the bedroom.

NINE

ALLISON RETURNED TO THE LIVING room and drank two more beers while she watched the first part of *Homecoming* for approximately the one millionth time. She kept having trouble with drowsiness, her head repeatedly falling back against the couch as she lost consciousness for minutes at a time. After this happened one time too many, she scooted to the edge of the couch and leaned forward in an attempt to keep herself awake. She wasn't sure why she was fighting it. It was beyond obvious her body needed rest. It'd been a stressful and tiring day. She was weary of everything. Probably some part of her figured this rotten day owed her at least a few faint moments of joy.

Another massive yawn stretched her mouth open so wide it made her feel like her jaw was on the verge of becoming unhinged. Her eyes felt bleary enough to make her want to gouge them out.

"All right," she said at last, leaning forward a little more. "Okay. I get the hint."

It was a losing battle no amount of coffee was going to help. Her plan at that point was to lumber off to bed and crash for however many hours it took to get her body back in something close to working order. At which point she would, of course, immediately commence binge-drinking again.

Instead of getting up, however, she grabbed her phone and checked it for the first time since dragging Cassie down to the basement. Her stomach knotted with tension when she saw the text from her supervisor. How long had it been since she'd even thought about checking in with anyone from work? Shit, how many fucking *days* had passed since she'd last logged into the work system?

That sick feeling in her gut intensified rapidly.

Oh, shit.

The message was significantly longer than the usual terse texts she received from her job. This one was a monolithic block of hateful text. Full paragraphs of accusatory shit. According to the message, three days had passed since she'd last logged into the system. Three whole days in the middle of the work week during which she was essentially missing-in-action.

Oh, fucking shit!

She had an in-person disciplinary meeting scheduled for the next morning, at 9 a.m. That this was one hour after her normal login time for work struck her as ominous. She was overcome with the sudden conviction she was about to be fired. A burst of intense panic made her heart speed up and her breathing quicken. Becoming unemployed wouldn't spell immediate doom. She had savings enough to get by for a while without supplementary income. For several months, at least, but eventually it *would* become a real problem. The idea of embarking on a new job quest in her current state was laughable. That was the thing that scared her the most about the whole situation.

Feeling slightly more sober now, she got up and started pacing about the trash-strewn living room. She tried hard to focus her scattered thoughts, but they kept trying to go in a thousand different directions at once. She felt close to total mental collapse until a single calming thought intruded, quieting the storm in her head.

In reading the text again, there was no overt suggestion of termination. Would they even bother calling her in for a face-to-face meeting if they were letting her go? She wasn't sure, but she had a hunch this meeting was intended more as a strong reprimand. A last-chance opportunity to listen to criticism and get her shit together. They might be putting her on probation, with the threat of termination if she didn't perform to expectations during that period. The more she thought about it, the more likely this seemed.

She had no choice but to straighten herself out, starting right now. No more drinking the rest of the day. No wake-up beer in the morning. She had to purge the poison from her system, at least until she had things under control again.

Allison staggered into the kitchen and put on a pot of coffee. When it was ready, she drank it all down over the course of the next hour and a half, then immediately put on another pot. She continued mainlining caffeine until she started to feel close to genuinely sober. It was a process that took hours. The whole time she felt jittery and it wasn't just from the caffeine. She was craving alcohol. It'd been quite a while since she'd forced herself to abstain for whole hours at a time. She didn't like it one bit, but she had no choice.

Even so, she started scratching at herself a lot, suddenly plagued by itchy patches all over her body. Between that and all the pacing around and muttering she was doing, she felt a bit like a hopeless drunkard in some old-time Hollywood movie, like Ray Milland in *The Lost Weekend*. The thought made her angry. She wasn't a fucking alcoholic, goddammit. This recent period of overindulgence was nothing more than a product of situational stress. It'd go away or ease up if she could just get herself back on track.

She made herself stay up until ten that evening. At that point she went to bed. She set her alarm for 6 a.m. and crawled under the covers. Falling asleep, however, took far longer than expected. Her mind was racing and she had a hell of a time making it slow down. She couldn't stop obsessing and worrying over everything that might go wrong at the meeting. She tossed and turned for at least an hour before finally drifting into unconsciousness.

Unfortunately, she woke up three times over the course of the night and each time she was forced to wage another battle against her worst impulses. At three in the morning, she told herself just one or two quick beers wouldn't be a problem. The beers would help her get to sleep and she'd feel better in the morning. Except deep down she knew this was total bullshit. She resisted the temptation and finally was able to nod off again. By the time her alarm jarred her awake, she'd managed a total of around four and a half hours of sleep.

Better than nothing.

She got up and stumbled off to the kitchen to put on another pot of coffee. Not being able to have her morning wake-up beer made her extra irritable, and she consoled herself with the knowledge that she could have as many as she wanted as soon as she got home from the meeting.

She went to the bathroom to take a shower, turning the water as hot as it would go. The scalding water felt good on her skin, as did the rising steam. She was overdue a good cleansing. In more ways than one. She felt more than filth sluicing away from her flesh. Her body was detoxifying, purging itself of all the bad stuff she'd been feeding it. Maybe this was exactly what she needed. Maybe it should be for more than just one day.

Something to think about, anyway.

After she emerged from the steam and heat, she felt refreshed and ready to face whatever the day had in store. Shortly afterward, she prepared a nourishing breakfast and made herself eat every bite. It was important that she feel as close to fully restored as possible before leaving the house. She was determined to show up for that meeting looking and feeling good.

The last step was physical presentation. She spent more time on her makeup and hair than she had in several months. Since her last day at that fateful horror con, in fact. She dressed in her nicest work clothes, donned jewelry she hadn't worn in ages, and added the subtlest touch of perfume.

Satisfied at last, she grabbed her purse and keys, locked the house up tight, and was on her way.

TEN

IF ALLISON'S CHEEKS HAD FELT any hotter, they would be in imminent danger of melting right off her skull. She imagined little globs of flesh dripping away and sizzling when they touched the table in the conference room. Her hands were under the table, clenched tight and trembling.

Dominick Harrison's brow knitted as he regarded her with apparent concern from the other side of the table. Dom was her supervisor. He was a youngish, heavyset man with a cherubic face. Allison couldn't help wondering if he was concerned for her sake or his own. Maybe he was afraid of her. Maybe he was doubting the advisability of a one-on-one meeting with the notorious black sheep of the company.

Maybe she wanted to tear his eyes out and feed them to him.

She swallowed with significant difficulty and relaxed her jaw muscles, unclenching her teeth. "Are you fucking serious? Did you really make me come down here just to tell me this fucking bullshit? *Seriously?*"

Dom grimaced. "Allison, let's be real here. We've been more than patient with you. And four weeks of severance pay is more than generous. You have me to thank for that, by the way. I went to bat for you. Normally you'd only get two. Or none, in especially egregious cases. Like . . . well, like this one."

Allison sneered. "You went to bat for me? I ask you again, are you fucking serious?"

Dom sighed and pinched the bridge of his nose, doing his best to look like a man striving hard for patience. "Allison—"

"Stop saying my name. I know my own fucking name, you fat fuck. No need to repeat it every other minute."

Dom flinched at her tone and rocked back some in his chair. "There's no point arguing about this. I'm sorry, but the decision is made. These things are never easy. I agonized over this, whether you believe me or not."

Allison snorted. "I believe you should rot in hell."

His expression hardened. "Twenty-seven, Allison." He leaned into her name, giving it an annoyed level of extra emphasis. "That's how many tardies and absences you've had going back to last summer. Twenty-fucking-seven. I've made a lot of allowances for you. You went through something truly terrible. But even you have to admit that's beyond the pale. At most companies, you would've been cut loose long ago, but, yes, I went to bat for you. I really fucking did."

She grunted. "But not anymore."

He nodded, sighing again. "No, not anymore."

"So that's it then? I'm just done here."

He shrugged. "I'm afraid so."

Exiting the building was like walking a gauntlet. She felt eyes on her from every direction, particularly as she moved past the cubicle farm where she once toiled away as a worker drone. She kept her eyes straight ahead the whole time, refusing to meet the gazes of any of her former colleagues. A giggle emerged from somewhere out there in cubicle land. The expression of mirth might have been about anything, maybe had nothing to do with her, but her gut told her otherwise. She didn't have to look at them to know there were a lot of smirking faces out there. They were all thrilled to see her gone for good. That she'd hardly been physically present in recent months didn't matter. As long as she worked for the company, there was always the chance she might be required to return to an in-person position.

But not anymore.

She banged through the door at the side of the building and hurried down the sidewalk to the parking lot. Her blue Chevy Cruze was parked in the fourth row back from the curb, the lot having been close to capacity by the time of her arrival. It felt a thousand miles away at first. She could still feel all those judging eyes on her, watching her through the plate glass windows. Part of her wanted to turn around and thrust both middle fingers in the air, but she thought better of the impulse, not wanting to give the people who hated her the satisfaction of seeing how upset she truly was.

After what felt like years of walking, she arrived at her car. The relief she felt when she fell in behind the wheel and yanked the door shut was overwhelming. Tears burst from her eyes as she set her purse on the passenger seat and started the engine. Her wish was to drive away as fast as possible, but she spent those first several moments behind the wheel too distraught to do so without immediately crashing into some other car. Maybe more than one. She had no choice but to let the tide of emotion run its course.

When she finally felt like she could take a breath without sobbing again, she looked at her tear-streaked face in the rearview mirror and said, "Well, that didn't go how I expected."

An understatement of massive proportions.

She'd talked herself into believing she wasn't being terminated today, weaving a whole web of what felt like flawless logic. This turned out to be a masterpiece of self-deception. Her attitude at the outset was sunny and positive. She was convinced Dom would see how motivated she was, how ready to turn everything around and become a model employee again. Because whatever else you could say about her in terms of personality, she'd always been good at her job. Excellent, even. So when Dom immediately made it clear they were meeting to discuss the end of her employment, it came as a brutal shock. She felt like she'd taken a heavy piece of lumber to the back of her head.

She wanted to scream and break things.

But not in view of the surveillance cameras in this parking lot.

She blotted tears from her face with a tissue, taking care not to smear her makeup worse than it already was. Another glance at the mirror revealed this as an impossible, pointless task. She wadded up the tissue and dropped it in her purse. Then she started the car, backed calmly out of the parking space, and drove away from her former place of work for the last time.

ELEVEN

LESS THAN A MILE AWAY was a truck stop where Allison for years made a daily habit of stopping in to grab a beverage and snack before work. On impulse, she pulled into the parking lot and went inside. Instead of getting a coffee or soda, she went to one of the coolers at the back of the store and grabbed a six-pack of Coors Banquet in bottles. She had lots of beer waiting for her back home, but that was an almost thirty-minute trip away and she was in no mood to hold out that long.

While waiting in the short line of customers at the counter, a gruff voice behind her said, "Kind of early for that, isn't it?"

She glanced around and saw a tall, bearded guy wearing a flannel shirt and ragged jeans. A beige trucker hat with a Peterbilt emblem was perched atop his head. Clutched in his right hand was a package of beef jerky and a tall can of Red Bull. She wasn't much into redneck trucker types, but he wasn't completely disgusting to look at.

She smirked. "It's the breakfast of champions."

He chuckled. "Think I've heard that one before."

"I'm sure you have. It's an old line."

It was her turn at the counter.

She paid for her six-pack and left the store without another word to the flirty trucker. Her Cruze was parked at the curb out front. Instead of getting in the car, she set the six-pack on the hood, took one of the bottles from the carton, and twisted off the top.

The trucker came out of the store and spotted her right away, frowning when he saw her guzzling from the bottle. "I might be wrong, but you strike me as a lady looking for trouble."

Allison took another big slug of beer. "You might be right about that. I might also be looking for someone to get in trouble with me."

The man grunted. "Is that so?"

She nodded. "It is. Think that someone could be you."

She said it like a statement, not a question. Like a challenge a real man couldn't turn down without calling his masculinity into question. Her intent was to achieve the opposite effect of yesterday's desperate and laughable attempt to seduce the beer delivery guy. She wanted to seem mysterious and alluring and not like a trashy, drunken wreck on the brink of a total breakdown. The public consumption of alcohol didn't quite line up with that, but she wasn't drunk yet at least. Also, she looked much better than yesterday, clad in her dark blue work dress, black stockings, and heels. And her hair was as close to perfect as it ever got. Take the cheap beer out of the equation and she looked almost classy.

The man glanced over to the large lot at the side of the building where all the tractor-trailer trucks were parked. Probably had his rig somewhere over there. Judging from the beef jerky and the can of Red Bull, he was probably done here and looking to get back on the road.

He looked at her again and sighed. "Wish I had the time, but I'm on a tight schedule."

Allison rolled her eyes. "Right. I think you're just afraid you won't be able to get it up. Maybe you don't like women."

A flicker of anger crossed his face. "You're wrong about that."

"Then prove it."

There was a motel across the street, the kind where you could pay either by the week, daily, or even hour-to-hour. A lot of the local transients and day laborers stayed there when they could scrape up the cash. It was also popular with hookers and truckers for obvious reasons.

Fifteen minutes after issuing her "prove it" provocation, Allison and the trucker were inside one of those rooms. It was exactly as seedy as she expected, with dingy walls and threadbare carpet in dire need of replacing. There was an unpleasant underlying smell no amount of air freshener spray could ever fully obscure. She didn't bother checking the sheets for faint semen stains, knowing they were almost certainly there.

She grabbed another beer from the carton after setting it on the rickety little table by the window. "Charming place."

He smirked. "Yeah, it's got a real 'home sweet home' vibe to it."

Allison twisted the cap off the bottle of Coors Banquet and flipped it across the room. She put the bottle to her mouth, tilted her head back, and drank the whole thing down in several huge glugs.

She dropped the bottle on the floor and sat on the edge of the bed. "You can do anything you want to me."

The trucker eyed her warily. "Lady, I really am on a tight schedule. No need to get crazy. This pretty much just needs to be a wham-bam, thank-you-ma'am kind of deal."

Allison shifted around on the edge of the bed, tugging up the hem of her dress and spreading her legs wide. "Are you sure about that? How often do you get this kind of offer? I mean it. Anything at all. Put your cock in any hole. *Every* hole, if you want. Come inside me. Come on my face. Choke me while you're doing it. Knock me around if it helps. Anything. Just as long as you fuck me as hard as you can. Make me feel something. I don't care if it's something bad."

The man looked more than wary now. He glanced around the room. At what, she had no idea. There wasn't much to see. He looked back at the door, his gaze lingering there a moment before returning to her.

She smirked. "You look scared."

He grunted. "Maybe I just don't want to get into anything too messy. See, now I'm thinking you're not just looking for trouble. You *are* trouble."

Allison laughed. "Pussy."

The man winced at her tone. "Okay, I'm out. No need to drive me back. I'll walk."

He started moving toward the door.

Allison got up and went to him fast, grabbing him by an arm. "Wait."

He turned toward her again with a sigh. "What now?"

She leaned into him, angling a thigh against his crotch. "How about the opposite of what I was saying? Is there anything you'd like done *to* you? Some secret fantasy you've never had the guts to request?"

He stared at her in silence for a few moments, the annoyed look on his face slowly turning into something else. Soon she felt his cock start to grow hard behind the crotch of his jeans. His breath quickened as his hands tentatively touched her waist. She raised up and nuzzled his neck, nipping lightly at it as she waited for him to work up the nerve to say what was on his mind.

When he finally did, she moaned softly and said, "Oh, yes. We can definitely do that."

Minutes later he was flat on his back on the bed with his quickly discarded clothes in a careless pile on the floor. She was astride him with his rigid cock inside her and her hands clamped tightly around his throat. His hands were behind him, his wrists bound together with one of her stockings. The other one was stuffed inside his mouth. She bucked and writhed against him, her hair flying, no longer perfectly coiffed. This went on for several minutes as she screamed in pleasure and verbally abused him, dredging up the most vicious insults she could summon from the darkest corners of her psyche. Vile, psychopathic things that went far beyond ordinary epithets or name-calling. His cock remained granite-hard as she continued to bear down harder on his neck, her thumbs pressing deep into the hollow of his throat.

Then he gagged and said something that sounded like a muffled plea for her to stop or ease up. Instead, Allison continued bucking atop him and digging her fingers in even harder. She saw his eyes open wide with alarm and abruptly shifted all her weight forward, trying her best to apply every ounce of it to the task of choking him to death.

Before that could happen, he managed to dislodge her. He was at last able to shift his weight around enough to roll her over. The only surprising thing about this was how long it took him to do it. He was bigger and stronger than her by a good margin. She laughed as he kicked and writhed away from her, struggling so hard he wound up rolling off the side of the bed. He cried out as he hit the floor, making her laugh again.

Allison scrambled off the bed and kicked him in the face when he tried to sit up. There was a crunch of cartilage as blood gushed from his nostrils. He flopped backward and howled in pain behind the stocking still wedged in his mouth.

There was no question she was in severe danger if she lingered here any longer. The man was at a temporary disadvantage, but that wouldn't remain the case much longer. She grabbed her dress and pulled it on over her head, not bothering with her underwear. The man was starting to sit up again as she stepped into her heels. She grabbed another bottle from the six-pack and smashed it over his head, opening a bloody gash in his scalp. The pungent stench of spilled beer made her crave a drink.

The trucker moaned as he rolled around in pain on the floor.

Allison grabbed her purse and keys and the remaining beers and went to the door, where she paused for one last glance back at the bleeding man. "Thanks for the fuck. I needed that. Ta-ta."

She opened the door, stepped outside, and hurried to her car.

TWELVE

A SILENT PASSENGER ACCOMPANIED ALLISON for much of her ride back home. She glanced at her rearview mirror and there he was, sitting in the back with the wide brim of that hat tilted low over his face, as always. His long, pointed chin and vulpine smile remained as creepy as ever, but seeing him there in her backseat did not terrify her. She remained calm as she sped down the highway.

She smiled. "Enjoyed that, didn't you? You were in there the whole time, watching me. I felt you feeding on my pain. Gorging on the intensity of my emotions. All the ugliness and hate. Reveling in my darkness because you made me this way, exploiting my personal damage, twisting and corrupting it into something far worse. This is what you really do, isn't it? The gifts are just a way in, how you keep me hooked. I'm a junkie and you're my pusher-man." She looked at the road now, still smiling. "It's okay. I'm not mad about it. I just want you to know that *I* know. I'm not like Mark. I'll never try to get away from you."

The Visitor was gone the next time she looked at the mirror. Or simply no longer visible. In a way, he was always with her, whether she could see him or not, that psychic connection always active.

The honking of a horn made her glance to her left. A car in the next lane was riding parallel to her Chevy Cruze. It was a white Elantra, recent model. The face of the young man in the passenger seat was twisted in a deliberately goofy expression, his eyes bugged out and his mouth stretched open wide. As she watched, he made his head wobble side to side. His purpose in doing this wasn't hard to deduce. He'd seen her talking—apparently to herself—and was saying she was a crazy person. It was stupid. For all he knew, she'd been on speaker phone with someone.

She flipped the guy off.

He tossed his head back and made a show of laughing like he'd never seen anything so funny. The driver of the Elantra hit the gas, blowing past her Cruze and then past the red F-150 ahead of her. Her hands tightened on the wheel as a violent fantasy took shape in her head. In the fantasy, she caught up to the Elantra and forced it off the road. She then pulled over and calmly got out while the boy who'd mocked her crawled out of the wreckage of the Elantra. There was a gun in her hand as she approached him. He rolled onto his back and held up shaky hands as he cried and begged for mercy. She sneered and shot him several times in the face before getting back in her car and driving away from the scene.

Any mild catharsis she derived from this was unsatisfactory. The reason why was obvious. Only a short while ago she'd indulged in an actual episode of bloody physical violence. Mere fantasies couldn't compare to the real thing, regardless of how vividly imagined. Also, she didn't actually own a gun, which made actualizing this particular fantasy impossible.

This train of thought inevitably led her to thinking about Cassie and Julia again. In all likelihood, both would be alive today if not for Julia's gun. Until that day, Allison hadn't even known her friend owned a firearm, or that she carried it around in her purse wherever she went. She had lots of good reasons to hate guns, but now she wondered if she should have one. For self-defense, of course. And for protecting her home. She thought of the smug face of the asshole in the Elantra.

And maybe for some other reasons.

It was something to think about, anyway.

She reached for the open bottle of Coors Banquet, but stopped short of lifting it out of the cupholder when she saw a cop car parked at the side of the road up on her right. There was no civilian vehicle parked in front of it, therefore no driver awaiting a ticket. She glanced at her speedometer and saw she was seven miles over the speed limit. Less than 10 mph over was generally considered a safe range, but she couldn't help feeling a sharp surge of paranoia. At least she wasn't drunk yet or swerving noticeably. Or so she hoped. She gave her brake pedal a light tap and kept her gaze straight ahead as she drove by the parked cruiser, willing herself not to immediately look at her rearview mirror.

She counted to five and then she looked.

The cruiser pulled away from the shoulder in the same instant.

Oh, fuck!

She immediately started rehearsing things she might say. Desperate, unlikely-sounding excuses. Nothing that would get her off the hook, she was certain. She wondered if she might be able to hurriedly hide the beer without the cop noticing what she was trying to do.

That didn't seem likely either.

Her heart felt like it was in her throat by the time the cruiser swerved into the other lane and blew by her. This was a massive relief, but she was badly rattled and didn't stop shaking until several more miles down the road. She remained jittery until she pulled into her driveway around fifteen minutes later. At that point, she shut the car off and sat behind the wheel until she could calm all the way down. She belatedly grabbed the open Coors bottle and started chugging the contents down, grateful she no longer had to worry about getting in trouble for it.

She leaned back in the seat and shook her head, laughing softly.

What a disaster of a day this was so far.

Well, fuck it all.

She wouldn't be venturing into the outside world again any time soon.

Grabbing her purse and the remaining bottles of Coors, she got out of her car, hip-checked the door shut, and went on inside. After locking the front door behind her—which felt like a symbolic banishing of the dreary reality that existed beyond it—she carried the beer carton to her bedroom and began the process of changing into comfier clothes. She put on white shorts and a black *Basket Case* crop top. It was cold and snowy outside, but warm in her house, and the interior climate was all that mattered. As long as she could easily manipulate that, who cared what it was like outside?

After changing, she carried the last bottle of Coors and the empty carton with her to the kitchen. She lingered there long enough to make and hastily devour a grilled-cheese sandwich. Breakfast wasn't that long ago, but all the morning beers made her hungry again.

Temporarily satisfied, she snagged a can of Natural Light from the fridge and went out to the living room. She felt a small pang of loss and regret upon spying her closed laptop on the coffee table. Never again would she use it to login for work, at least not with her now former employer. The feeling faded, however, when she saw the Blu-ray case propped up against the front of the VCR. She was positive it hadn't been there prior to her departure.

Curious, she set the can of Natural Light on the coffee table and hurried over to the old TV. She snatched up the case and gasped in shock and delight when she saw the cover.

The name of the movie was *The 13th Friday: Jason Lives Again.*

Allison jumped up and down and danced around the room, laughing and laughing as she felt the darkness brought on by the disastrous early part of the day slide off her like a dead old skin.

THIRTEEN

THE SENSE OF ALMOST TRANSCENDENT elation Allison experienced in the wake of her unexpected discovery did not begin to ebb until several hours later. By then she'd already watched the "new" *Friday the 13th* movie straight through twice with a gap of only a few minutes between viewings.

According to copyright information on the back of the case, the movie was originally released in some alternate version of 1999. This Blu-ray, however, was a collector's edition issued in 2019 through Scream Factory. It was packed with extra features. She was almost as excited about that as the movie itself. Most of the alternate reality discs she'd received thus far were bare bones, with scarcely any extras included. It would be fascinating to dive into the behind-the-scenes history of a movie that didn't even exist in her world.

Despite her excitement, she was more than a little confused. She'd made no recent special requests of The Visitor, not since the arrival of alternate-world Cassie. All the other gifts she'd received were things she'd explicitly asked for—begged for, in some cases. The movie's sudden appearance in her home was a mysterious thing, though she did wonder if it might be some special treat or reward for enduring so much hell just lately. This notion went against everything she thought she understood about The Visitor, but she could think of no other explanation. It was worth remembering, however, that the true motivations of any interdimensional being were beyond simple human comprehension.

She decided against wasting any additional time fretting over it and instead settled in with some more beers to start watching. The pre-credits intro sequence was longer than standard and surprisingly light on bloody thrills, especially considering what gory FX extravaganzas the other alternate *Friday* movies she'd seen were. The first several minutes after the credits were also comparatively bloodless and ploddingly paced. In addition, some of the acting wasn't up to the elevated standard of *Homecoming* or even *Reckoning*. She began to fear she was seeing her first dud of an alternate *Friday*. At that point she just hoped it would wind up better than *Jason Takes Manhattan* or *Jason Goes to Hell*.

To her surprise, the film took a sharp turn for the better around the twenty-minute mark. Jason killed a large-breasted blonde bimbo and her football player boyfriend in the woods in shockingly brutal fashion. The setup for the scene was so cliche it felt like an intentional homage to the early '80s classic era of slashers. In this film, however, the killer was bigger and stronger than ever, and these particular murders involved some bare-handed limb dismemberment. The bimbo died after her boyfriend, spraying an astonishing amount of blood everywhere as she staggered and spun around with her arms torn off. Jason caught up to her and twisted her head off her shoulders, triggering another over-the-top gusher of gore. This sequence prompted Allison to pick up the case and read the text on the back again.

She nodded, smiling.

Of course.

This was a "restored" unrated edition.

From that point forward, the gruesome killings came at a frenetic pace and many were satisfyingly creative and cruel. The preppy good girl she initially assumed would be the requisite "final girl" of the flick perished halfway through, when she was dragged naked out of a shower and then down a hallway until she was tossed down a flight of stairs. She managed to crawl into the nearby kitchen, where Jason caught up to her and stabbed her with at least a dozen different kitchen implements until she was wobbling around like a human pin cushion. He finished her off by ramming a rolling pin deep down her throat, a moment that made Allison gasp and say, "Holy fucking shit."

A short newspaper blurb on the cover called the movie "The meanest *Friday*."

They weren't kidding.

In terms of plot, *The 13th Friday* was middle of the pack as far as the franchise went. There was no doubt *Homecoming* was still easily the best-written film in the series. But what this movie lacked in that area it more than made up for in sheer brutality. Allison loved it and by the time it was over knew she had to watch it again immediately.

Throughout both viewings, her beer consumption continued at a rapid clip. Her accelerated intake was a dual byproduct of blowing off steam and happiness over the movie. By about the midpoint of her second viewing, she was close to being blitzed out of her mind. Her eyelids started to droop and she struggled to stay awake, though she managed the feat of keeping her eyes open until the end through sheer determination. Then she gave up and allowed herself to pass out right as the closing credits began to roll.

By the time her eyelids fluttered open again, she was slumped down in the middle of the couch with her face tilted toward the ceiling. Her head was pounding and her mouth had that fuzzy-thick feeling that always came with those first waking moments following an episode of overindulgence.

Allison groaned as she sat up straighter and took a look around. It was clear she'd been unconscious for hours. Judging from the darkening of the room, it was late afternoon at least. Only a faint bit of sunlight filtered in through the window blinds now. A greater abundance of empty beer cans littered the already crowded surface of the coffee table. There were more on the floor now, too. The ever-present stench of stale beer was also worse. She figured she'd spilled some during that sloppy period right before she passed out. It'd been a while since she'd given a shit about the mess, but it was getting to be too much. It might be a good idea to walk through here with a trash bag and scoop up most of the empties and discarded food containers. That way she could start over with a clean-ish new slate before beginning her next binge.

First, though, she needed to take care of something else.

She got up and stumbled off to the bathroom.

While sitting on the toilet, she felt fuzzy-minded and woozy. Her eyes still had that raw feeling that came from being overly tired. She blearily wondered if she should head off to bed for a few more hours of sleep before attempting to clean up or start drinking again. Probably so. She was feeling good about this plan when it dawned on her there was something she was forgetting.

Something important.

Her eyes abruptly widened.

Oh, fucking hell.

She hurriedly finished in the bathroom and ran out.

FOURTEEN

SHE UNLOCKED THE DOOR TO the basement and immediately cringed at the thick odor of piss and shit when she opened it. Her guest was still alive down there in the darkness. She could tell from the constant, low-level moaning. The woman sounded like a dying animal on the side of a road, lingering in torturous fashion after being run over by a car.

Allison was tempted to close the door and allow nature to take its course. Unless she intervened, it was a process that shouldn't take much longer, judging from what she was hearing. She only hesitated because she knew there was a chance she was wrong about how far gone the woman was. She might linger for days yet, for all Allison knew. It wasn't like she had any previous experience in this area. Maybe she should get on her phone and look up how long it took the average person to starve to death or die of thirst.

She replayed that last thought in her mind, shaking her head.

Jesus Christ. What have I become?

Her capacity for empathy wasn't nearly what it once was. As long as The Visitor remained a presence in her life, her humanity would continue eroding away a little more each day until she had no conscience at all. This only bothered her when she was confronted with extreme examples of the consequences of that erosion.

Like this one.

Setting aside her reservations about seeing Cassie in her current miserable state, Allison flicked on the light switch at the top of the stairs and commenced a careful descent to the bottom. The overpowering odor of bodily waste made her put a hand to her mouth to stifle a gag.

The crate was against the back wall of the basement, in a space once occupied by an old storage trunk now crowded into her small attic, along with other relics of the past. It was a heavy-duty steel construct designed to prevent escape from or destruction by large, aggressive dogs. She'd purchased it online. The cheaper type of easily disassembled crate sold at pet stores wouldn't suit her purposes.

Cassie lifted her head off a blanket she'd balled up and used as a pillow. Her eyes were puffy and red. The volume of her moaning increased dramatically when she saw Allison approaching. She raised her head higher and tried to talk but could only gag. After making some hacking noises in her throat, she tried again and wailed in complaint: *"You were gone for so long!"*

Allison shrugged as she stopped a few feet short of the crate. "I've been busy. I also just sort of forgot, if you want to know the truth."

"It feels like it's been weeks!"

Allison rolled her eyes. "Don't be so dramatic. It's only been a little over twenty-four hours."

"I thought you were never coming back!"

Allison winced, taken aback by the volume her guest was generating now. She suspected it was fueled by surging anger. There was terror and distress in that voice, clearly, but there was also an intense level of rage.

She moved a step closer to the crate, glaring down at her guest through the slats at the top. "Watch your tone. And lower your fucking voice. You're mad. I get it. But I'm the one in charge here, remember? Can you behave, or do I need to get the broom again?"

Cassie whimpered. "I'm sorry. Please don't hurt me again. I'm hungry. I'm thirsty. Please."

Allison's face twisted with disgust as she leaned closer to do a more thorough examination of her guest's physical state. "You're also filthy. I should probably pull you out of there and clean you."

The woman's backside was smeared with feces. She appeared to have endured a case of explosive diarrhea at some point during her long period of confinement in the darkness. Some of the tangled blankets were also heavily stained and would need to be thrown in the trash or burned up in the fire pit out back. The situation wasn't helped any by the metal brace still locked into place between her ankles. She hadn't been able to move around easily the entire time, which surely worsened her state of misery by a considerable amount.

Cassie sniffled and looked up at her with pleading eyes. "Could you please just let me take a shower? I'll be good, I promise. I won't try to fight you or anything."

Allison shook her head. "Allowing you to shower or clean yourself sounds like something I might let you do as a reward for good behavior. The problem, Cassie, is you've been nothing but bad, so you'll have to endure the indignity of being washed like a baby again."

Cassie rose up on her knees as best she could and screamed: "*Fuck you! You're a fucking monster!*"

She grabbed hold of the slats at the front of the crate and started trying to shake them, a useless gesture of rage and defiance that produced little discernible noise. The slats didn't rattle like the bars of a jail cell in an old movie. The construction of the crate was too sturdy for that.

Allison kicked the front of the crate, eliciting a yelp of pain from Cassie. "Stop whining, you stupid bitch. You're your own worst enemy, you know that? Things could get so much better for you if you just started cooperating."

"*Go to hell!*"

Allison's face drained of all outward emotion as she stared at Cassie in absolute silence for a period of minutes. She then remained silent as she turned away from the crate and headed back across the basement to the staircase. Behind her, Cassie wailed louder than ever, hurling histrionic insults in between pathetic pleas for help.

The woman's furious desperation moved her not at all.

Once she reached the top of the stairs, she flicked off the light.

Then she closed and locked the door again.

FIFTEEN

AFTER SUFFERING THROUGH HER GUEST'S self-pity tantrums, Allison decided to go to bed as she'd originally planned. The woman in the crate was in rough shape, no doubt, but it was clear she hadn't weakened to the point of imminent demise. She was grateful the woman's screaming was only faintly audible outside the basement when the door was closed because having to listen to that all night would get annoying before long. Putting on some white noise while she slept would obscure the rest of it easily enough, as she'd learned from experience these last couple weeks.

She fell asleep shortly after six in the evening. When she woke up just over four hours later, she felt a lot better. In physical terms, at least. There was still a black cloud hanging over her from losing her job, but there was nothing she could do about that until at least the following day. In truth, she strongly doubted she'd commence a job hunt tomorrow or the next day, maybe not even for weeks yet. There was definitely no point in worrying about it right now.

Besides, she had other, more immediate problems to consider. Like what to do about Cassie. She gave the matter some thought as she had a steaming hot cup of coffee in the kitchen. A plan began to take shape. Unfortunately, it would require leaving the house again, but if she wanted to do this right, she had no choice.

She returned to her bedroom and dressed for the colder temperatures outside. That done, she went to the bathroom, opened the medicine cabinet, and sorted through various expired prescription bottles until she found the one she wanted. There were three Ambien pills left in the bottle. She took them with her to the kitchen and stuffed all three into a wad of raw cookie dough.

Then she went back down to the basement and crouched in front of the crate, offering the cookie dough to Cassie, who eyed it with wary reluctance.

Allison scowled. "You're hungry, right? You led me to believe you were starving to death. Or should I just throw this out?"

In the end, Cassie's hunger won out. She accepted the "treat" and quickly gobbled it down. As soon as it was gone, she immediately began begging for more. She wanted water, too, was so desperately thirsty.

Allison ignored all this and departed the basement.

She donned a coat, activated her alarm system, and left the house. The nearby Walmart was set to close at 11 p.m. She had just over half an hour to get there and procure the items she needed. After getting there with just over fifteen minutes to spare, she made a beeline for the hardware department, where she was quickly able to locate everything on her shopping list.

By the time she returned home, it was after eleven.

She carried the brand-new double-bit axe and large tarp down to the basement. Her guest was unconscious and snoring as Allison descended the stairs. On the off-chance Cassie was playing possum, she kicked the crate multiple times. She didn't stir in the slightest and never stopped snoring. Just to be extra cautious, she slid the axe into the crate and poked at her back with a corner of the blade. She pressed the blade a little harder against the bare flesh, piercing it slightly this time. A tiny bead of blood welled out of the hole as she withdrew the axe.

Still no reaction whatsoever.

Allison set the axe aside and spread out the tarp. Fully unfurled, it covered a good two-thirds of the floor, which should suffice. With that done, she removed her coat and hung it on the post at the bottom of the staircase, well out of the potential range of forthcoming blood spray. Unless she was underestimating, which she hoped wasn't the case. It was her nicest winter coat and she'd hate to get blood all over it.

She returned to the crate, removed the padlock, and opened the door. Crouching now, she stuck her head through the opening and unlocked the leg shackles, carefully removing them along with the brace. She backed out of the crate long enough to toss the shackles aside. The chains and wrist shackles she'd remove after she had the woman situated on the tarp. She reached in again and grabbed hold of her ankles, gripping them tight as she carefully pulled Cassie out. Up close, the stench of her feces-stained flesh was even worse, making her gag.

Allison let go of Cassie's ankles after dragging her to the approximate center of the tarp, which bunched up some. She spent a couple minutes pulling at an edge of tarp until she had it fully straightened and spread out again. At that point, she used another key to unlock and remove the wrist shackles. The longer length of heavy chain looped twice around her waist was attached to the wrist shackles. Fully removing it required flipping Cassie onto her side more than once, first to one side and then the other. Once she'd finally accomplished all that, Allison began to get to her feet.

Cassie screamed as she opened her eyes and rose up off the floor, clamping a hand tight around Allison's throat. Her grip was strong and crushing, like a band of steel. Allison spluttered and tried twisting out of the woman's grip, but she was too off-balance and couldn't do it.

Cassie shook her like a doll and screamed again. "*I'm going to kill you!*"

Allison looked around wildly, searching for the axe.

It was propped up against the back wall of the basement, several feet directly behind Cassie. She caught only fleeting glimpses of it as Cassie closed both hands around her throat now and continued to squeeze harder and harder, apparently determined to deliver on her threat of murder. That strong grip was a shocking thing. By all rights, the woman should be incapable of mounting an attack of this ferocity, weakened by hunger and thirst. If she didn't want to die here in the next few minutes, she needed to start fighting back just as savagely.

She stopped clawing at the squeezing hands and drilled a fist into the middle of Cassie's face. For a second time that day, she saw blood gush from an opponent's nose. She wasted no time delivering a second punch to the same place with even greater force. Cartilage crunched. Cassie's hands came away from her throat as the woman staggered backward and crashed into the wall behind her.

Allison sucked in ragged gasps of air.

But the moment of reprieve was short-lived.

Cassie saw the axe and grabbed it, raising it over her shoulder as she pushed away from the wall and approached Allison with a sneer on her face. "Well, look at that. You look scared. Not so tough now that we're on equal footing, are you?" She faked a swing of the axe, making Allison shriek and stumble backward a step. Cassie laughed. "Did you think I was dumb enough not to realize you put something in that cookie dough? I puked that shit up as soon as you were gone, bitch."

Allison grunted, a sound tinged with the smallest hint of admiration. "Good job not reacting when I pricked you with the axe. That's some next-level shit. I don't think most people could've done it."

Cassie smiled. "I'm not most people. If your Cassie was anything like me, you should've guessed that."

Allison nodded. "I fucked up. Obviously."

"You sure did, bitch." Cassie shook sweaty strands of hair out of her face and adjusted her grip on the axe, making Allison cringe in anticipation of a swing that wouldn't stop in mid-arc. "So now that I'm not locked up—now that I'm the one with the fucking advantage—let's try doing things another way. I'm gonna give you one last chance to not be a piece of shit, against my better judgment."

Allison frowned. "How do you mean?"

Cassie's smile faded. "What I mean is that, unlike you, I'm not a monster. I don't want to hurt anybody if I don't have to, not even you. So unless you want me to change my mind and chop your fucking head off, here's what's gonna happen. You're gonna get in that crate. And then—"

Allison surprised her with a giggle. "Don't be ridiculous. I'm not doing that."

Cassie scowled. "Yes, you are. And I'm gonna lock you in there like you did to me. Just long enough to clean myself up, steal some of your clothes and money, and get the hell out of here. As soon as I'm a safe distance away, I'll put in an anonymous call to the cops, let them know you're in need of rescue."

This time Allison didn't just giggle.

She laughed like Cassie was saying some of the funniest shit ever.

Then she said, "You don't get it, you dumb cunt. It's like you haven't listened to a thing I've told you since you got here. Do you think you're just gonna assimilate into this world and lead a regular life?" She shook her head. "Even if you tried, it wouldn't work. You're a person, yeah, a human being, but in one important way you're just like all my other gifts from The Visitor. You don't belong in this world. As long as you're in my vicinity—in my *possession*, being real about it—you're okay. But if you go out into the world, people will sense you don't belong. They'll fixate on you. Follow you. Try to keep you for themselves. I don't know why. It's just how this shit works. And The Visitor won't be happy with me if I let you get away. I'd be forced to hunt you down and bring you back."

"*Bullshit.*" Cassie said the word with palpable venom, her eyes flashing as the axe handle shook in her grip. "You're a liar. A fucking liar. All you've done is lie to me from the beginning."

Allison shook her head, a sad look of commiseration on her face. "That's just not true, Cassie, and I think you know it."

Cassie's eyes welled with tears. "You fucking awful bitch. You talk about me being okay as long as I'm with you like I don't know what you had in mind for me when you came down here this time." Her gaze moved in a pointed way from the tarp to the axe and back to Allison's face. "Or do you want to lie about that, too?"

Allison shrugged. "I won't lie. I was planning to do exactly what you're thinking, but only because you've done nothing but fight me and frustrate me. Maybe we could agree to try again, on a level of mutual respect? I admit I could do better in that area. Think about it. No more crate, no more chains. As long as you stay here with me and don't try to leave."

Cassie sniffled. "You know this is wrong. Deep down, you do. Why not just send me back to my world, where I belong?"

Allison allowed a silent beat to elapse.

Then she laughed. "Because I don't *want* to."

Cassie stared at her in wide-eyed disbelief for a moment.

Then she shook her head. "Okay, then."

She lifted the axe higher and charged at Allison.

SIXTEEN

WHAT HAPPENED NEXT WENT DOWN so fast Allison didn't have time to be afraid. Her would-be assailant's bare feet slid on the slick tarp and the axe flew from her hands as she toppled backward and crashed to the floor. Instinct kicked in at that point. Allison hopped over Cassie, snatched up the axe, and gripped it low on the handle with both hands. She spun about and saw Cassie starting to get up again. Planting her feet like a baseball player standing at home plate, she pivoted with her hips and swung the axe with all her might. Cassie was upright again at that point, but she didn't have time to react. The heavy axe blade punched deep into her abdomen. Her eyes went wide and she tried to scream, but the explosion of pain appeared to overwhelm her.

Allison held tight to the axe handle as she began to move swiftly in a circular motion, forcing Cassie to spin with her with the axe still buried deep in her gut. Allison laughed, feeling like a demented child engaged in a macabre playground act. Instead of Spin the Witch, it was Spin the Dead Bitch. That thought made her laugh even more heartily.

She kept up the spinning game until Cassie's legs began to weaken and buckle. Maintaining her grip on the handle, she allowed the woman to first sink to her knees and then flop onto her back. Then she planted a foot on her waist and ripped the blade free of the dying woman's body.

Allison looked down at her, sneering. "Does that hurt? It looks like it hurts."

Cassie's quivering lips moved, but no words emerged.

Allison laughed again. "Thanks for landing about where I had you in the first place. It's a big help. Truly."

She raised the axe high above her head and allowed gravity to assist her as she brought it down again, the blade chopping into Cassie's body with much greater force than the first time. This time the blade crunched into the space between her bare breasts, an area of her body that offered significantly greater resistance than her soft belly. The blade nonetheless penetrated inches deep into the chest wall. Cassie's limbs spasmed and a hacking sound emerged from her throat.

The placement of the axe made Allison think of a scene from *Friday the 13th: The Final Chapter*, the one where the character played by Barbara Howard dies from an axe wound to the same part of her body. This happens when strong-ass motherfucker Jason Voorhees throws the axe *through* a door, fatally impaling her. Sara, the character in question, dies with a towel wrapped around her torso, affording her a level of modesty not shared by alternate-world Cassie as she met her demise.

After allowing herself a few additional moments to admire the similarities between this real act she'd perpetrated and a moment from one of her favorite pieces of entertainment, Allison worked the blade free again, though it took more effort this time, being buried in a mass of tough muscle and bone. She then went into something of a frenzy, hacking away at the fresh corpse until she'd severed the feet, arms, and head. It was harder work than she expected. Making things more difficult was the blood running out of the limb stumps. Even in her shoes, it made moving around on the tarp slippery. Despite the work she'd done thus far, she was far from satisfied. Reducing the body to pieces of a more manageable size would require a tool of a different type.

Like a chainsaw.

Unfortunately, she didn't *have* a chainsaw.

It was a problem she could easily remedy with another trip to Walmart, but that would have to wait until tomorrow.

Or . . . maybe not?

She frowned, thinking about it.

Because, yes, she didn't have a chainsaw, but she *did* have a battery-operated reciprocating saw she sometimes used to trim tree branches on her property. Not nearly as powerful as a chainsaw, of course, but she'd used it to cut through branches as thick as her forearm, a task it accomplished with speed and ease. It *might* have just enough oomph to get the job done. As a bonus, it wouldn't be nearly as noisy as a chainsaw. In hindsight, it struck her as funny how she went right to chainsaw as the obvious tool of choice without considering anything else. That was the mind of a horror fan for you.

Allison put her coat back on and went upstairs, this time leaving the basement door open. And why not? There was no current need to worry about disturbing sounds emerging from that part of the house.

After donning gloves and boots, she went outside and approached the small tool shed that occupied a rear corner of her backyard. She unlocked the shed's door, flipped on the light, and stepped inside, locating the saw in under a minute.

Taking the saw, an extra battery pack, and the optional power cord with her, she went back inside and got to work again.

SEVENTEEN

THE RECIPROCATING SAW FUNCTIONED acceptably well over the next couple hours as she set about the task of reducing the corpse to an assortment of much smaller pieces. Before beginning, she removed every stitch of clothing. This would be incredibly messy work and any clothes she wore would be ruined.

She was finally at the point where she was ready to start cutting up the body when she realized she was on the verge of missing a prime opportunity to capture a pivotal moment in her existence on video. So back upstairs she went to her bedroom, where she unplugged the camcorder and removed it from her dresser. Taking the camera and an extra blank VHS tape with her, she returned to the basement.

After setting up the camera and positioning the lens at an optimal wide angle, Allison started the recording. "Hi, guys," she said cheerily, smiling and waving at the camera. "Yes, I'm naked, but we're all adults here, so let's be mature about it. So, this is crazy, but I went and did something extra impulsive. Like, I had no plans of doing anything like this until a few hours ago. Anyway, it's better if I just show you. But brace yourselves, okay?"

She stepped aside, allowing the camera an unfettered view of the splayed-out and partially dismembered corpse. Five seconds later, she stepped back into view, cringing for the camera. "I know, I know, totally fucked up, right? I mean, technically, it's murder, I guess?" She shrugged, smiling again. "But is it, though? I kind of don't think so. Not really. Cassie was already dead in this world. This chick was, like, a *fake* Cassie. An inferior duplicate. Killing her wasn't like killing a real person. It was like taking an axe to a life-sized doll. A defective one, at that. Her brain wouldn't work right and I was tired of trying to fix her."

Her expression shifted as she appeared to think over what she'd said, the smile slowly fading, giving way to a petulant frown. "Whatever. It happened and I couldn't take it back even if I wanted to, which I fucking don't. The important thing is that now I have a gigantic fucking mess on my hands. And now you get to watch while I attempt to deal with it."

She moved out of view just long enough to grab the saw, stepping in front of the camera again a moment later to display the tool. "Here we go," she said, her sunny smile returning. She clicked the saw's trigger, making the blade whir a little. "Mmm, I dig that sound."

She moved away from the camera and dropped to her knees at the dead woman's side. Depressing the trigger again, she moved the reciprocating blade into position and applied it to the dead flesh for the first time. Her first order of business was cutting open and displaying the entire abdominal cavity. She then began a process of removing as many internal organs as she could, work that sometimes required more applications of the whirring blade. The slimy, slippery organs went into a large plastic bucket lined with a trash bag. Stomach, liver, pancreas, intestines, kidneys, and more. Extracting the heart and lungs required temporarily setting aside the saw and going back to work with the axe. She widened the fissure in the chest wall and cracked open the ribcage. The bucket was getting pretty full by the time she dumped the chopped-up remains of Cassie's heart and lungs inside it.

The work was as messy as she'd anticipated and then some. She had a great deal of blood and gristle spatter on her torso. There was more blood on her face. Several times she had to stop and wipe blood from her eyes with the back of her arm. At least she had the foresight to tie her hair back before starting. A hair net and goggles would've made things even easier, but those were items she hadn't anticipated needing.

She said as much to the camera, adding, "So I'm not as prepared as I'd like, but give me a fucking break. This is my first total corpse dismemberment. It is absolutely one of those learn-as-you-go kind of deals."

Severing the legs from the torso was the next thing she did. The first step was removing the lower legs just below the knees. This was where the reciprocating saw first had to work extra hard. The saw vibrated severely and she had to grip the handle tight with both hands to keep the blade from bouncing away from the bone. There were a few moments where she feared the saw might not be up to the task after all, but she maintained her tight grip on the handle and kept applying the pressure. She swept the lower legs aside with a squeal of triumph each time they finally came loose. Separating the upper legs from the trunk of the body proved an even harder task, but eventually she got it done.

There was still work to do, but she was sore from exerting herself so hard and decided to take a little break. She stripped off her latex gloves and dropped them in the bucket. Then she trudged her way upstairs and went into the kitchen and grabbed a beer from the fridge. She popped the tab on the can and walked out to the living room. The phone she kept losing track of was on top of the closed laptop. She picked it up and started scrolling through her social feeds while sipping beer, stopping a few seconds later as she realized she didn't care to peruse the inane shit people were saying tonight. Politics, riots, race relations, mass shootings, and pandemic news. All that outside-world fuckery. Instead, she spent some time taking selfies of her naked, blood-spattered body. She thought they looked hot. Not that she'd ever actually share them with anyone.

Well, *probably* not.

But maybe . . .

Perhaps she should look into becoming a horror-centric cam girl now she was out of a job. Maybe create an OnlyFans account and do it there. Call herself GoreGoreGirl666 or some other cheesy shit like that. Unless . . . did the platform have any kind of restriction against violent imagery? She didn't know, but she could look into it. If not, surely she could find some other, even dodgier site that would let her get as gruesomely freaky as she wanted. She was nobody's idea of a traditionally hot model, but she had a decent body and she knew for a fact there'd be no shortage of guys into what she had in mind. It was a niche audience, no doubt, but she was positive she could be as savvy about exploiting it as anyone else out there.

The out-of-nowhere idea wasn't anything she'd previously considered, but now she found herself utterly captivated by it, to the point that for a time she forgot all about the messy job she still hadn't finished. She wandered back into the kitchen for another beer as she continued to mull it over, getting excited about all the possibilities, the clothes and costumes she might wear, as well as the various blood-splattered scenarios she'd concoct for her audience. Never mind that said audience was still entirely imaginary at this point.

Midway through that second beer, she came out of her reverie and realized she needed to get back down to the basement and get back to work with the reciprocating saw and a few other implements from the kitchen. The work was time-consuming, but she couldn't just leave it for another day.

After all, she didn't want the meat to spoil.

EIGHTEEN

THE REST OF THE WORK took nearly another two hours. While it wasn't as physically demanding as the first phase of the process, the thoroughness it required exhausted her. When she was finally finished, she took a shower to wash all the blood and gristle off her body. She was fascinated by the way the blood at the bottom of the tub stained the water bright red. Watching the redness slowly swirl down the drain made her feel like she was the star of a much bloodier version of the shower scene from *Psycho*.

After the shower, she got dressed and resumed her usual habit of slugging back beers and watching nothing but horror movies. She kept at it until shortly after dawn, when she finally staggered off to bed and fell right asleep atop the rumpled sheets.

Her mind was fuzzy in the usual post-binge way when she regained consciousness at just shy of three in the afternoon, temporarily devoid of anything like coherent thought. She'd fallen asleep facedown, but now she rolled over and groaned as she rubbed at her bleary eyes.

Then an image popped into her head.

Cassie's corpse on the basement floor.

In many bloody pieces.

A wave of sickness washed over her as she realized the gruesome images in her head were actual memories and not fragments of some twisted dream. Her stomach clenched and the bile rushing up into her throat made her scramble quickly to the side of the bed, where she opened her mouth wide and puked onto the floor. Her face turned sweaty as she heaved a few more times.

As the worst of the sickness receded—at least temporarily—she pushed away from the edge of the bed and fell onto her back again. She hugged herself as she started shivering, overcome with abject horror and disgust at what she'd done. Vile, sick, inhuman things. She felt an urge to walk outside and throw herself in front of the first speeding car that came down the street. Being turned into bloody roadkill was the least of what she deserved for her monstrous acts. More gruesome images came floating up from the depths of memory, torturing her with vivid and undeniable proof of her vileness. She was reprehensible, an utterly irredeemable excuse for a human being.

I'm a piece of shit, she thought, tears flooding her eyes. *That's what I fucking am.*

Hot on the heels of this savage self-condemnation came another thought, an even more startling one.

Hold on, what's happening here?

Why do I feel like this? Why do I feel anything at all?

After months of steady erosion to the point where it seemed to no longer exist, her conscience was back. She felt like her old self, her humanity fully restored. Her mind flashed backward, revisiting all the terrible things she'd done to alternate-world Cassie, even before killing her. Like how she'd caged her like an animal and made her sleep in filth. The beatings. The food deprivation and the endless psychological manipulation. All leading up to brutal murder. She'd committed fucking *atrocities* and she'd been basically okay with all of it, barely ever batting an eye.

She launched herself off the bed when her stomach twisted again and rushed to the bathroom, making it as far as the sink before she had to stop and puke again. Hot tears spilled continuously from her eyes as she hacked and coughed, feeling more miserable than ever before in her life.

Then she froze, tensing up.

He was behind her.

The Visitor.

She felt him there even before she looked at the mirror and saw the partially hidden blur of his face looming over her shoulder. The fast-flowing tears dried up almost immediately and the crushing wave of self-loathing abated. She sniffled and wiped moisture from her face. Her briefly functional conscience was inactive again, turned off like a light switch.

"What was that? Punishment of some kind? You mad at me for destroying your gift?" She grunted. "That's it, isn't it? I would've thought you'd like that. The darkness and sickness of it."

She let out a long exhalation of breath as she felt him reach into her mind and communicate with her in his unique way. No actual words, per usual, but as always, the shape and texture of his thoughts became known to her.

"Okay, I'm sorry, but she was getting on my nerves and I was tired of her shit." She smirked. "Next time I'll ask for your permission first, I promise. While we're at it, I don't like that you can turn my normal human feelings off and on like that. It's fucked up. I thought that part of me was just dead."

The Visitor loomed behind her a moment longer, but there was no further communication.

Then he was gone, with no response to her complaint.

Motherfucker.

Allison went off to the kitchen, returning to her bedroom moments later with a wad of paper towels and a plastic grocery bag. She cleaned up the pile of puke next to her bed as best she could and stuffed the wad of soiled towels in the grocery bag. Getting up, she tied off the bag and carried it back to the kitchen, where she shoved the bag into the overflowing trash can. She almost left it at that, but impulsively hauled the Hefty bag out of the can, tied it off, and replaced it with a new one. Getting the bag out of the can required more exertion than usual after over a week of shoving things into it long past the point of timely, sensible replacement.

She left the bulging, tied-off old bag on the floor next to the trash can and went to the sink to wash her hands. After drying them off, her stomach made a noise of hunger, surprising her. She didn't often feel famished after puking her guts out, but this time was a serious exception.

She was starving.

So Allison went to her refrigerator and opened the door, peering in at all the packaged pieces of Cassie meat. There were so many of them there wasn't much room left for anything else. Except her beer, of course. This was a natural consequence of so thoroughly carving the meat from the woman's bones. She'd used up all the plastic wrap and large sandwich bags at her disposal. More packages of Cassie were wrapped and taped-up in pieces of brown wax paper. There were so many of them she'd have to be careful to not let it go bad. Anything that didn't get used by the end of the week would have to go in the freezer, but she considered that a good problem to have. Having such an abundance of fresh meat meant she wouldn't have to put in a grocery order of any significant size for a while.

Allison smiled.

More money for beer.

She opened the freezer door and looked in at Cassie's severed head, which was wedged into a back corner in a bed of ancient frozen vegetable packages to keep it from tipping over. One way alternate-world Cassie differed from the version she'd known was her hair. Whereas *her* Cassie had raven-black locks cut in a classic Bettie Page style, this troublesome other version had worn her hair in a punkier, rock-chick style dyed a bright shade of scarlet. If she'd kept the bitch around, she would've forced her to grow her hair out longer and dye it black. Too late now.

She flipped the freezer door shut and took a package of Cassie thigh meat out of the fridge, along with a can of Natural Light. Opening the package, she spread the wax paper out on the counter and poked at the meat with an index finger. It looked and felt tender and juicy. She licked the tip of her finger and felt her stomach growl again.

Using her sharpest knife, she cut off a respectable chunk of the meat and dropped it into a skillet on the stove along with a pat of butter. The rest of it she rewrapped and returned to the fridge. She drank her wake-up beer and tended to the meat as she cooked it, marinating it in yummy spices and sauces. The scent of the meat as it sizzled in the skillet made her mouth water in anticipation of greedily devouring it. She flipped the big chunk of meat over a few times, watching it turn brown. When she deemed it ready, she cut off the burner, scooped the meat onto a plate, and carried it over to the kitchen table.

Before settling in to eat, she decided it was time for her first social media post in months. The only problem was she once again couldn't remember where she'd put her phone. She went into the living room, but didn't see it on the coffee table. A check of her bedroom also came up empty. Then she went to the basement, which was still a horrible, bloody mess. At some point soon, she'd have to figure out what to do with Cassie's remains, but that could wait. She still had a meal to eat and it would start getting cold if she didn't get back to the kitchen soon.

Just as she was on the verge of abandoning the search for the phone, she happened to glance into the big bucket of organs and guts and there it was. She fished it out and hurried back upstairs. In the kitchen, she cleaned blood and unidentifiable goop off the phone and snapped a picture of her meal. She posted it to Twitter and Instagram, adding the caption, "Having a friend for lunch."

This prompted a giggle.

Posting the picture this way made her feel bold and naughty at the same time, but in truth she wasn't risking much. She'd killed someone who wasn't from this world, which meant no one here was looking for her. She was a non-entity. Also, this world's Cassie being half a year dead meant she could dump the remains any old place without worry. They might well be discovered, but so what? If some CSI lab matched the DNA with the original Cassie, the cops would have one hell of a mystery on their hands, but it was one they'd never be able to solve.

She tested the meat and, as she suspected, found it was no longer as warm as she preferred. Bummer. She popped it in the microwave for a minute, tested it again, and found the heat level acceptable. It could stand to be a touch warmer, but she didn't want the meat to get too tough from the microwave. She wanted it juicy and as close to fresh-tasting as possible.

Finally settling in to eat, she sawed off a chunk of the Cassie steak and forked it into her mouth. She groaned in astonished, almost sexual pleasure, stunned by the tender, savory flavor. Another bite produced the same reaction, making her squirm in her chair. She kept sawing away at the meat and gobbling it down, feeling gluttonous as she ate faster and faster.

After wolfing down the last bite, she set her fork on the plate with a clatter and leaned back in the chair. "Holy shit. Oh my God."

Cassie was one of the most deliciously amazing things she'd ever tasted, a delicacy absolutely beyond compare, at least in her experience. She felt full and satisfied in a way she hadn't in a long time. This was without doubt something she wanted to experience on a regular basis. She couldn't help feeling amused. Was it her destiny to become a full-time convert to cannibalism?

Maybe so.

This didn't bother her in the least. She was completely okay with becoming a real-life Hannibal Lecter or Drayton Sawyer.

Pushing back from the table, she got up to carry the plate to the sink.

And that was when the banging on her front door started.

NINETEEN

ALLISON JUMPED WHEN SHE HEARD the sound, it was so loud and abrupt. The plate slipped from her fingers and shattered when it hit the floor. She barked a curse and felt a surge of intense anger. The banging on her door continued, which did nothing to lessen her rage. And now there was a shout from the porch, one imbued with apparent concern. She had a small house. In all likelihood, whoever was out there being an obnoxious pest had heard the commotion coming from her kitchen.

Taking care to avoid cutting up her bare feet on the ceramic plate shards, she went out to the living room and then into the foyer, where she peeked through the eyehole at the front door. There were two men out there in suits and short haircuts. One gray suit and one black. They had a hard, officious look to them. Right away she pegged them for cops.

Her suspicion was confirmed an instant later when the one in the gray suit took out a detective's shield and held it up close to the eyehole. The fucker probably heard her breathing hard from the other side of the door. She was still gripped by red-hot anger, but now there was a little fear in the mix.

Motherfucking cops. Always deducing shit. Fucking assholes.

The one in the gray suit said, "Hilliard police. We'd like a word, Ms. Cook. Please open the door."

Allison had trouble swallowing for a moment. Her voice was

74

hoarse when she was finally able to speak. "Just a minute!"

Her heart was racing and she was trembling. Fear overtook anger. Any cop who saw her like this would instantly know she was guilty of something. She needed to get a handle on her nerves fast and show some level of composure when she opened the door. The problem was she knew she couldn't reasonably delay stepping outside for long, not without arousing suspicion.

"Be right back! I need to get my keys."

She moved away from the door before they could respond.

Panic gripped her as she ran out of the living room and down the hallway to the bedroom. She checked herself out in the full-length mirror next to the dresser, looking for telltale signs of blood anywhere on her clothes or body. There was nothing incriminating she could see. Well, okay, the *Bloodsucking Freaks* crop top she'd donned at some point last night probably wasn't ideal attire for chatting with cops. She hurriedly peeled it off, yanked open a dresser drawer, and started rooting through her T-shirts for something less garish.

No, wait.

That would take forever.

She ran to her closet instead, swept aside some hangers, and found a plain black top that would suffice. After putting it on, she went back out to the hallway, where she paused long enough to close and lock the basement door. She almost dropped her keys when the knocking on her door recommenced.

"*I'm coming!*"

Resisting the urge to scream epithets at them was not easy.

Making everything worse was her total bafflement concerning this unexpected visit from the pigs. She'd just been thinking about how killing Cassie should be no big deal from a standpoint of legal repercussions and, as far as she could see, that should still be the case. No one else in this world even knew this version of Cassie existed. The men on the porch *couldn't* be here for anything having to do with her.

It was just impossible.

So what the fuck?

Thinking about it in a logical way calmed her down some as she arrived at the door. This visit had nothing to do with her killing and butchering a human being last night. She felt confident in that fact. Perhaps some other crime had been committed elsewhere in the neighborhood and they were checking with neighbors to see if they'd seen or heard anything suspicious.

Sure, that had to be it.

She was sliding her key into the deadbolt lock when she remembered the trucker from the motel. That was, what, two days ago? Longer, maybe? She thought it was two days, but it didn't really matter. Either way, more than enough time had passed for the cops to look into the incident. There was probably surveillance footage of her with the trucker at the truck stop and the motel. The possibility that the man might report the incident never crossed her mind in any serious way until now. She'd assumed he had far too much masculine pride to ever admit to being roughed up by a girl.

Then again . . .

Her mind flashed back to that morning. She thought about how she'd kicked him in the face, breaking his nose, and she remembered how it felt when she smashed the beer bottle over his head. Most of all, she remembered the blood, flowing freely from his nose and the gash in his scalp. Though she'd quickly put it out of her head afterward, as if it'd been no big deal, in retrospect it'd been quite the violent assault, and that wasn't even taking into account her attempt to choke him to death.

Okay, so she'd done a little more than "rough him up."

Was she possibly in some real trouble here?

Fuck.

One of the men on the porch—probably the belligerent fucker in the gray suit—banged on the door again.

"Ms. Cook, we have a warrant for your arrest in the murder of Robert Anton Levine. Please surrender peacefully."

Murder?

Fucking *murder!?*

Robert Anton Levine was undoubtedly the name of the trucker because it otherwise meant nothing to her. She knew she'd hurt the son of a bitch, but figured none of it was anything that couldn't easily be fixed at the ER.

Apparently not.

What the fucking fuck?

She took the key out of the deadbolt and backed off several steps as the banging commenced yet again. The one cop started yelling again, but her thoughts were in too much of a frenzy to process any of what he was saying. She was starting to feel like a cornered animal. The likely path of her immediate future started playing out in her head like scenes from a movie scarier than anything she'd ever seen.

Arrest. Jail. Someone would discover the mutilated remains in her house. At that point the mystery of alternate-world Cassie wouldn't matter. The undeniable truth was there was a hacked-up dead bitch in her house, one she'd partially devoured. She'd be charged for that murder, too, as well as for corpse defilement. The evidence against her in both cases was overwhelming. She'd spend the rest of her life in fucking prison. A more horrible fate she could not imagine. You probably didn't get to watch horror movies in jail. She'd never see *Homecoming*, *Reckoning*, or *The 13th Friday* again.

Her eyes filled with tears.

The banging on the door intensified.

Allison ran into the kitchen and grabbed a steak knife. She cried out as one of the smaller ceramic plate shards pierced the bottom of her right foot. Droplets of blood trailed her as she hurried out of the kitchen and down the hallway to the bathroom. She locked herself in and pushed the overfilled clothes hamper against the door. It wouldn't keep the cops out for more than a few seconds if they tried to bust in, but she didn't know what else to do. Any effort to flee the house was probably doomed to fail. She was barefoot, underclothed, and there was at least a foot of new snow on the ground.

She faced the mirror and put the knife to her throat, daring herself to slice open her jugular vein. She trembled and cried, terrified by the prospect of dying within the next few moments. Never in her life had she been so fucking scared, but the grim thought of decades of misery in prison scared her even more.

She started to press the blade against her flesh.

The banging from the living room got louder than ever.

They were trying to bash the door open now.

Allison took a calming breath and removed the knife from her throat. She redirected her gaze to a bottom corner of the mirror and did her best to focus her thoughts. It was difficult because she knew she only had seconds left to attempt this desperate move.

She took another deep breath and worked on her concentration.

"You don't want to lose me. I'm the most willing host you've ever had. I will never resist you. Feed from me as freely as you wish forever. Do with me what you will. Just, please . . . please take me away from this place."

The cops broke through the front door.

She heard agitated voices and footsteps in the hallway.

They were a dozen feet away now, calling for her.

THE UNSEEN II

Then even closer.
Sighing, Allison put the knife to her throat again.
Then she slipped into darkness.

TWENTY

AND FROM DARKNESS SHE EMERGED, standing by the side of a two-lane road in some rural area. The road was bordered by an overgrown field on one side and a wooded area on the other. She had no solid sense of where this place was, but it was a safe bet she wasn't in Hilliard anymore. Or anywhere in Ohio, for that matter. There was no snow on the ground, for one thing, and though it was cold enough to make her uncomfortable in her shorts and blouse, she gauged the temperature at several degrees north of freezing. That was good news considering her lack of weather-appropriate attire, but she hoped she wouldn't have to spend a significant amount of time walking around out here in her bare feet.

She looked around and saw only curving stretches of faded asphalt heading off in either direction. There were no buildings or other signs of civilization. Without her phone, she had no easy way of getting her bearings, a situation she lamented before realizing she was better off without the device. The one advantage she had over Hilliard law enforcement right now was her inexplicable removal to some new and possibly far away location, one likely to remain a mystery to them for some time unless she did something stupid to give herself away. Like use her phone. Fortunately, that wasn't an option now.

Spying a glint of sunlight on something silver nearby, she turned toward the object and saw the steak knife she'd grabbed during her brief detour into the kitchen of her house a few minutes ago. She scooped it up and looked around again, still seeing a whole lot of nothing. Shaking her head in mild dismay, she focused her thoughts and tried sending them to The Visitor. *Thanks for getting me out of there. I appreciate it. I really do. But couldn't you have sent me somewhere more convenient? Like somewhere with people, maybe? Or behind the wheel of a car with a key in the ignition?*

Allison waited for anything resembling a response for a few moments, but none seemed forthcoming. The usual strange tingle at the back of her neck she felt whenever the entity was about to put in an appearance never happened. It seemed she was being left to her own devices for the time being.

So be it.

All she was sure of at the moment was she couldn't just stand here forever, shivering in the chilly air. She was on her own with no one to help her and no means of artificial guidance. No internet. No GPS. The only thing she could do was pick a direction and start walking. And hope for the best.

So that's what she did.

She'd gone only about a quarter mile down the road when she heard a car approaching from behind her. Instead of immediately turning toward the rising sound of the engine, she kept walking as she shifted her grip on the knife's handle, turning it so the blade was pressed against the underside of her wrist. Keeping it hidden until she knew she wouldn't need it seemed wise, given how little she knew about her changed circumstances.

Her bare feet crunched on the gravel at the side of the road as she continued to plod forward with her head down. As the car drew closer, an inner debate waged in her head. She was all alone and vulnerable in this strange place. Yes, she'd turned herself into a killer just recently, but that willingness to commit violence on its own might not be enough to protect her. Should she turn around and flag down this car and risk falling into the hands of a predator? On her home territory or anywhere near it, she'd never seriously consider it, but this was a highly unusual situation, to say the goddamn least.

She stopped walking as the car slowed to a stop next to her in the road. A window slid down and a male voice spoke. "Do you need help?"

Allison was still facing forward, hadn't even looked at the guy or his car yet. "Maybe. Are you some kind of creep?"

He chuckled. "That's a matter of opinion, I guess. Depends who you ask. But if you mean am I a murderer or rapist, the answer is no, I'm not."

Allison sighed. "I guess I'll have to take your word for it."

She turned toward the car.

It was a late-model Lexus. Dark blue and immaculately clean, shiny in the afternoon sunlight. Either it was brand new or it'd been through a car wash recently. No scratches or dings anywhere. A luxury car in such pristine condition didn't seem like it belonged out here, traveling along a lonely back road in the country. Unless, of course, this area wasn't as rural as it seemed at first glance. For all she knew, a more populated area might be mere minutes away by motor vehicle.

The guy poking his head out the open window wasn't bad-looking. He had a mass of thick but short and neatly-cropped black hair atop his head and a matching beard. His face was blandly handsome and he possessed a degree of natural charm. Didn't mean he *wasn't* a sexual predator, of course. He could be Ted fucking Bundy reincarnated for all she knew.

"So how can I help you? Do you need a lift somewhere?"

Allison shrugged. "There a town somewhere nearby? And maybe a Walmart or something where I can get some clothes?"

The man frowned. "Ah . . . yeah. Yeah, there is. And I'll take you there if you want." He indicated the empty front passenger seat with a tilt of his head. "I'm Isaac, by the way. And you are?"

"Allison Lecter."

"Well, hop on in, Allison."

Keeping the hand with the knife turned away from him, Allison went around to the other side, where she opened the door and dropped into the passenger seat. The door closed on its own, which she found annoying. She wondered if she'd be able to open it easily again if she needed to bail out suddenly. There was a lot about this situation that made her uneasy, but the idea of resuming her barefoot walk down the road wasn't an especially enticing one.

The car started rolling forward again, neither occupant saying anything for the next few minutes. The silence made Allison twitchy and she did some nervous shifting around in her seat. A wild impulse to lean over and stab Isaac came and went. She didn't feel comfortable in his presence, but killing him now probably wasn't the best solution. Not while the car was in motion, anyway. The guy gave her a weirdly contemplative look as the Lexus went around a tree-shaded bend in the road. As the road straightened out, a roadside clearing came into view.

The car began to slow down.

Allison frowned. "What's happening?"

Isaac glanced at her and smiled, but didn't say anything. He guided the Lexus to a stop at the back of the clearing, angling it in such a way that anyone passing by in the street would not easily be able to see inside the vehicle.

Allison sat up straighter in her seat and took a look around. "Why are we stopped here?"

Isaac shut off the engine, popped his seatbelt off, and reached down to touch a button at the side of his seat. There was a whirring sound as the seat moved backward several inches. He shifted toward her slightly. "Let's talk."

Allison grunted. "Let's not."

His smile faded some. "I'm doing you a favor. The least you can do is humor me a minute."

Allison again considered stabbing him. It'd be easier and less dangerous now with the car parked. Also, he'd made an easy and tempting target of himself by putting some room between his torso and the steering wheel. With nothing to impede the arc of the knife, she could bury the blade deep in his belly before he even knew what was happening.

It was an interesting option she might yet utilize if things took a bad turn, but a new sense of caution stayed her hand for the time being. This was the only person she'd met since being transported to this place she still knew nothing about. An impulsive act of murder at this early stage could complicate things in a lot of ways, perhaps even destroy this second chance she'd been given before she could take proper advantage of it.

She sighed. "Fine. So talk."

There was a touch of irritating smugness in Isaac's expression now. "That's more like it. There's some things I'd like to understand about your situation. You're not dressed for the weather. You've got no shoes on and you were walking with a little bit of a limp. There's no house in the immediate area you might have run out of and I didn't see any broken-down cars before running across you. Yet I have this strong hunch you've just escaped from some kind of trouble. Like within the last few minutes. So do you mind explaining how that's possible?"

Allison shrugged. "That's an impressive sense of intuition you've got there, Isaac, because you're dead on the money. I *did* escape a troublesome situation a few minutes ago. What happened is, some cops came to my house in Ohio to arrest me for murder. Looked for sure like I was flat-out fucked, but then this interdimensional being called The Visitor intervened and transported me to this place, wherever the fuck it is."

Isaac squinted at her, pondering her words and studying her face for a moment. Then he shook his head. "You know what? I've changed my mind. I don't need to know your story. Save the imaginative rambling for someone more gullible. Let me get a look at that foot."

Allison frowned. "What?"

"Your hurt foot. The one you were favoring when I saw you walking. Let me see it."

Her frown remained in place as she gave him a longer, silent look. His expression was bland, betraying no trace of lasciviousness. At least not yet. She popped her own seatbelt off and turned in the seat until she was fully facing him, at which point she lifted up her foot for him to see. He took gentle hold of her ankle and guided the foot toward him for a closer look.

"Hmm. This could get infected if you're not careful. It needs to be cleaned and bandaged."

Allison grunted. "All the more reason to get me to that Walmart as soon as possible."

He made a noise of acknowledgment but continued staring at the sole of her foot. The pad of his thumb lightly rubbed the area near the wound. She studied his face carefully as this happened, smirking when she saw him suck moisture from the corners of his mouth. He was nervous and trying not to show it. She flexed her toes and felt his hand tremble.

So you're one of those. Okay, then.

"Look, I'm gonna be blunt. I don't have any money for clothes or anything else. If I give you a foot job, will you buy me the things I need?"

His face turned red, but he nodded and said, "Yes. Of course. Anything you want."

She sighed. "Well, whip it out then. Let's get this over with."

He smiled and reached for his zipper.

TWENTY-ONE

ONE BENEFIT OF GETTING A total stranger off with her foot instead of just fucking him was the reduced risk of further complications down the road. There was no chance of getting an STD or becoming impregnated, which was nice. Given the profoundly fucked-up state of her existence, she couldn't imagine a more horrifying development than the latter. Not that she'd ever harbored any strong desire to give birth. Even prior to the erosion of her humanity, she'd known she wasn't meant for that kind of life. She was already too broken, too socially incompetent to ever be a good mother. The way she saw it, she was doing society a favor by recognizing her shortcomings in this area and taking the necessary steps to ensure such a disaster never occurred.

Now, of course, other recent deeds of a far darker nature had undoubtedly negated any prior spiritual goodwill she'd earned. Soon enough her parents, former coworkers, and other acquaintances would hear about the things she'd done. The basic details were lurid enough to elevate the story beyond the level of ordinary murder. The corpse mutilation and hints of cannibalism alone would ensure that. Then factor in that she was a young female perpetrator and obsessed horror fan and suddenly you had a story so sensational the media might feast on it for weeks or months to come, perhaps even longer. She couldn't give a shit what her estranged parents or phony online "friends" thought about her. The only thing that did bother her a little was how the horror community would perceive her. She knew from personal experience how horror fandom negatively colored the way the public perceived people who loved the genre. It was massively unfair. Most genre fans were normal, loving people who weren't nearly as messed up as she was.

They were going to hate her now.

It sucked, but there was nothing she could do about it. Short of turning herself in, maybe, but no way in hell was she doing that.

By the time they arrived at the Walmart—no more than a ten-minute ride from that little roadside clearing—she'd already deduced they were somewhere in Tennessee. The license plates she saw on most of the vehicles they passed gave that away. She wouldn't have guessed her location based on Isaac's accent, which had only the smallest hint of southern flavor, and even that she only detected in retrospect.

She was intensely self-conscious as they entered the store, being the only person barefoot and in shorts. A store employee gave her grief over the lack of shoes shortly after they walked through the entrance, but the situation was defused when Isaac calmly explained why they were there. A basic pair of gray sneakers was procured, purchased, and donned in short order.

Her self-consciousness did not fade as she threaded her way through the various racks and tables in the women's clothing department. People kept looking at her and making her uncomfortable. These weren't just casual glances, either. Several people, male and female, openly stared at her as she selected her outfits. She detected lust in a few of those gazes, including from at least one of the women. This was a strange enough thing on its own. Because she had a slim build and wasn't completely hideous, she did get a few semi-interested looks now and then when she was out in public, but nothing like this level of attention. The lustful ones were ogling her like she was Miss Universe strutting around in a string bikini rather than the Plain Jane she actually was. What she saw in the eyes of most of the people staring at her, however, was just a weird intensity she couldn't attribute to anything in particular. It couldn't have anything to do with the crimes she'd committed. Not nearly enough time had passed for the national media to pick up the story. Her paranoia kicked in big time anyway.

She was tempted to drop her selections and run screaming from the store. The main reason she didn't was Isaac's presence. She didn't like him much—he *had* revealed himself as a low-level form of sexual predator, after all—but right now he was the only thing resembling a lifeline available to her. She didn't know if he'd actually protect her if someone tried to grab her or attack her, but he was at least some kind of buffer.

Satisfied at last with her selections, Allison suggested they head to the front of the store to check out. She wanted out of this place before all the staring from strangers drove her crazy. Isaac agreed to this and they started heading in that direction. Then Allison stopped him with a hand on his elbow, having thought of something else she needed.

She didn't know where she was going after she and Isaac parted ways, but she would need something in which to keep her new clothes and other things she might acquire. An inexpensive travel bag, perhaps. So they reversed direction and headed for another part of the store. Along the way, Allison happened to glance into a large bin filled with cheap Blu-rays.

She came to a stop with a startled gasp and snagged a Blu-ray from the top of the huge pile of discs. Her jaw dropped open as she stared at the cover, her hands shaking as she repeatedly read the title to be sure it was real and not a product of her imagination.

The movie was *Friday the 13th Part IX: Homecoming*.

Isaac looked confused. "Um . . . are you all right? You look like you're having some kind of episode."

She thrust the Blu-ray into his hands. "What's the title of this movie?"

Isaac tilted his head, his look of confusion deepening. "Uh . . . can you not read?"

Allison rolled her eyes. "Of course I can fucking read. But I've been through some crazy shit and I need independent verification of something so I can know I'm not losing my goddamn mind."

Isaac still looked dubious, but shrugged. "It's one of those Jason movies. The ninth one."

She snatched the disc case from him and clutched it protectively against her chest. "Could you please get it for me? I'm sorry, I know you're already doing so much, and I appreciate all of it, but this movie means so much to me. Like, more than almost anything. So . . . please?"

He shrugged. "Well, sure, I guess. I mean, it's only five dollars. What's the big deal about this old-ass movie anyhow? It's on TV a lot every year at Halloween time. I'm not much into horror shit and even I've seen *Homecoming* a bunch of times."

Allison frowned. "I could tell you, but it's complicated."

I already sort of have, she thought, *but you thought it was a joke.*

She took another look around, becoming troubled as she saw how many people were still staring at her. She was sure some of them had followed her from the clothing department, with others joining in along the way. Once again, they were making no effort to hide what they were doing. The scrutiny in no way felt friendly. These people wanted to get at her. They wanted to put their hands on her, to hold and possess her. The desire wasn't even entirely sexual, though that was clearly an element of it for some of them. It was more like a helpless compulsion. She believed they'd already be converging on her if not for the public setting, and she wasn't sure how much longer even that consideration would hold them back.

She looked at Isaac, her eyes wide with panic. "We need to get out of here. *Now.*"

"What about your travel bag?"

She grimaced. "Maybe you could get me one later. Can we please just go?"

Isaac appeared to take full stock of the evolving situation for the first time. At first he just looked puzzled as he surveyed the staring faces, but soon enough the first stirrings of fear dawned in his expression.

"Um . . . what's going on?"

She grabbed him by an arm again and quickly led him through a gap in the crowd. Isaac stumbled a few times but managed to keep his footing as she maintained a rapid pace, cutting through the shoe department and then through the various clothing areas in the middle of the store. A glance over her shoulder confirmed what she suspected. They were being pursued by several of the staring people, who all looked desperate to not lose sight of her.

As they neared the checkout registers, Isaac took out his wallet and said, "Don't slow down. Keep going toward the entrance."

She saw him take multiple hundred-dollar bills from the wallet before tucking it away again. There would be no normal checkout process, then, no pausing to individually scan each item and pay the designated proper price. Instead he'd attempt to bypass all that by pressing an overabundance of cash into the right hands.

Having little other choice but to go along with this brazen

disregard for protocol, Allison blew past the self-checkout registers with the basket of clothes and the Blu-ray of *Homecoming*. A security guard attempted to stop her at the entrance, but then Isaac was there to press another hundred-dollar bill into the man's hand. The guard relented and they were outside within seconds, moving fast in the direction of Isaac's car. Allison risked another quick glance over her shoulder and saw a crowd of people streaming out of the entrance, following after them. Some were running.

Oh, shit.

Allison started moving faster and Isaac quickened his pace as well. He took out his electronic key fob and unlocked the Lexus when they were within twenty feet of it. Allison ran the remaining distance, yanked open the passenger side door, and dove in, tossing the shopping basket into the backseat. The steak knife was where she'd stashed it before heading into the store, under the seat. She grabbed it and gripped the handle tight, ready to start slashing away at anyone who tried to get at her.

Isaac got in and started the car, hitting a button to lock the doors. His face registered surprise when he saw the knife. "Where did that come from?"

"Never mind that. Get us the fuck out of here."

Some of their pursuers were now in the spaces between cars, pounding on the windows and shouting at Allison. A bearded man dressed in camo took out a gun and screamed some unintelligible threat. Not that Allison needed to know his actual words. The fucking gun said more than enough. He was standing right in front of the Lexus, pointing it at them through the windshield.

Isaac said, "This is crazy."

Allison couldn't argue with that.

Isaac put the car in gear and hit the gas. The Lexus shot forward, slamming into the armed man and pinning him against the bumper of the big pickup truck in front of them. Camo Guy's mouth opened wide as he screamed in pain. More importantly, he lost his grip on the gun. It slid off the hood of the Lexus as Isaac changed gears and started backing out of the parking space. The other obsessed ones continued pounding on the windows. A few got behind the Lexus and tried to block its path, but to Isaac's credit he didn't let this impede his efforts to get away from the mob. He just kept the vehicle in motion and eventually the crazy people trying to block their way were forced to move aside. Some of them were already running away as Isaac changed gears again, presumably in search of their own cars to continue giving chase.

Allison pulled on her seatbelt and braced herself. "Burn rubber, motherfucker."

This was another request Isaac was happy to oblige.

TWENTY-TWO

THE HIGH-SPEED FLIGHT CONTINUED until they were several miles gone from Walmart. Even after Isaac shifted back to a less breakneck speed, he wasn't ready to stop taking extra precautions to foil any still ongoing pursuit. This included abrupt reversals and turns down side streets. He was driving like he thought he was in some spy or heist movie from the 1970s. Ordinarily, Allison was not a fan of being a reckless driver's passenger, but in this case, she was okay with it.

As Isaac steered them through the unfamiliar streets, she sat slumped down in her seat, with her head turned away from the road. After the scary incident at the store, she had to assume anyone who saw her might fall victim to the same helpless compulsion as those others. By now, of course, she knew what was causing the obsession. She just didn't know what to do about it.

She didn't belong here. That was the problem. The people here sensed it on a primal level. She was something rare and special. An alien among them. This was why sharing The Visitor's gifts was forbidden, or at least strongly discouraged. The same compulsion led to the deaths of her only real friends when they were exposed to the *Homecoming* videotape.

This world was an alternate reality, some parallel universe where things were largely the same as where she was from, but not exactly. Some of those differences were minor things, such as, for instance, deviations in the history of her favorite slasher franchise. She had no doubt there were cultural differences and historical divergences of greater significance, but she hadn't been here long enough to familiarize herself with them. It would probably all be fascinating as hell if she could exist in this world in a normal fashion. Based on her experience so far, however, that didn't seem possible.

When she made her desperate appeal for removal to some other place, she expected The Visitor to know she meant somewhere else within her own world. Another state or country, whatever, but she hadn't specified that and now here she was, removed from one mess only to find herself mired in another one. She needed to reestablish contact with the creature and request an immediate return to her own world. Life as a fugitive there might become difficult, but it'd be preferable to what she was dealing with now. At least back home she could disguise herself and attempt to lead some kind of manageable underground existence. Changing her hair color and adopting a new name wouldn't help her in this place, unless she could come up with a way of short circuiting the compulsion caused by her otherworldliness, and as far as she knew, that wasn't possible.

Still scrunched down in her seat, she frowned as she thought of something else, barely noticing as Isaac reduced the car's speed. She was wondering if The Visitor might have had some hidden motive in bringing her to this world. He didn't bring her here by accident. She was sure of that. He was an entity able to move objects and people between planes of existence. Everything he did was by design, with some purpose in mind. He would've been well aware of the difficulties she'd face here. Was she being taught some kind of additional lesson about the consequences of failing to heed his rules? If so, she would have to express contrition in some convincing way, show him how committed she was to never fucking up again.

The car rolled to a stop.

There was a soft electric hum as the driver-side window slid down.

Allison sat up straighter and frowned as she watched Isaac reach out the window and punch a code into a keypad mounted on a stanchion. Ahead of them was a gate that began to roll open when he punched in the last digit. Beyond the gate were rows of storage units with white metal doors. Isaac drove through the opening and the gate automatically closed behind them.

"What are we doing here?"

Isaac kept his gaze straight ahead as he steered the Lexus through the large, maze-like facility, which consisted of many rows of identical units. "Only place I could think of to get out of sight and try to figure things out without being harassed by insane strangers." He glanced at her as he continued to make his way through the facility. "I've never seen anything like what happened back there. It was madness. And it was you they were trying to get at. Do you have any idea why?"

Allison sighed. "I know exactly why. You just wouldn't believe it."

"I'd believe just about anything at this point," he told her, grunting as he brought the Lexus to a stop in front of a unit indistinguishable from any of the others save for the number above the door—1991. "Hang tight. Be right back."

He got out of the car and unlocked a padlock hanging from a hasp. Seeing the lock made her think of Cassie, the version she'd imprisoned in her basement for two weeks before murdering and partially devouring her. The mental association made her uneasy. Yes, this guy had helped her a little, but in truth he was still an absolute stranger, one who'd coerced a sexual favor from her before providing help.

She considered bolting from the car and making a run for it as she watched him roll the door upward and venture into the storage unit. The only reason she didn't was she had no clue what to do or where to go after she scaled the perimeter fence and fled the facility. There was no one else in this world she could trust, no way she could just blend in with a society largely populated with people who wanted to possess her or hurt her. Or both.

Isaac came back to the car and peered in at her. "Come on, let's talk in there."

Allison eyed the inside of the unit warily. "What's wrong with talking in your fucking car?"

He shrugged. "Like I said, for privacy. So no one can see you."

Allison slowly craned her head around. "We're the only ones here as far as I can see."

He sighed. "Yeah, for now. But this is a big place. People are in and out all the time. Would you like to try explaining things out here in the open, where someone might come along at any moment, or would you rather do it in there, where we definitely won't be disturbed."

Allison frowned harder.

She studied the interior of the unit, looking for red flags, obvious warning signs of a dangerous situation. All she saw was metal shelving along the walls. The shelves were crowded with long white boxes. At the back of the unit was a table upon which sat stacks of envelopes, express mail boxes, and what looked like an electronic postal scale. She saw nothing of an overtly alarming nature, but she remained reluctant to get out of the car.

She looked at Isaac. "Why here? Why not back at your place?"

A pained look creased his face. "Because I'd rather not have to explain you to my wife and two young children."

Allison gave him a scornful look. "You're fucking married? You have *kids*? For fuck's sake."

A hint of red crept into his cheeks. He said nothing.

Allison sneered. "So where's your wedding ring?"

He dug into a pocket of his black slacks and held up something for her to see. The gold ring glittered in the sun for a moment before he slid it back into place on his left ring finger. "I took it off when I saw you walking down the road."

She gave him a look of disgust. "You sleazy motherfucker."

He shrugged. "Never claimed to be perfect. So . . . do you want to talk and see if I can figure out some other way to help you? Maybe I *am* a sleazy motherfucker, but I don't see anyone else rushing to your aid at the moment."

He had a point there.

Still clutching the steak knife, she got out of the Lexus and followed Isaac into the storage unit. He pulled down the metal door, turned around, and invited her to take a seat in a swivel chair pushed against the table in back. She pulled the chair away from the table, spun it around, and dropped into it. This she did despite not liking the way it allowed Isaac to loom over her, but there was a weariness dragging her down, compelling her to sit. She kept the steak knife held in front of her, though, glaring at him in a pointed way.

"You get out of line, I will fucking stab you a hundred goddamn times. Understand?"

He nodded, looking a little amused. "I understand."

"I'm not kidding. I will gut you like a pig and laugh while doing it."

The little glint of amusement disappeared. "I believe you."

Allison took a look around before allowing her gaze to settle on him again. "What is all this shit?"

He looked slightly sheepish. "This is my side hustle. I sell comic books and old vintage magazines on eBay. Used to operate out of my house, but Tanya resented the space it was taking up. I considered renting an office in town, but this was cheaper."

"Tanya is your wife?"

Isaac nodded.

"Show me a picture."

Isaac took out his wallet, removed a photo from one of the pockets, and handed it over. The picture showed a smiling blonde woman with salon-styled hair and fashionable clothes. She stared at the picture in silence for several moments, trying and failing to comprehend.

She handed it back. "That bitch is fucking gorgeous."

Isaac tucked the photo away and returned the wallet to his back pocket. "I know."

Allison didn't give one shit about this man beyond how he might be able to help her, but a strange bitterness overcame her anyway. "I look like shit compared to her. Even at my absolute best, she'd make me look like a fucking gutter rat. If you've got that waiting for you at home, why would you ever bother with my sorry ass?"

His face contorted as he appeared to search for words he didn't have, his features then going slack again as he gave up. "To be honest, I don't know. Something just sort of . . . came over me."

Allison sighed wearily.

The revelation was deflating in a way she hadn't anticipated. Up to this point, she'd fooled herself into believing this guy was somehow immune to the helpless compulsion triggered by her alienness. Turned out he just wasn't as immediately obvious about it, probably because he had the early advantage of no competition for her attention.

Seeing that she was lost in thought, he cleared his throat. "You said you'd explain what happened at the store."

Allison nodded. "And I will, but you're not going to believe a word of it. I already sort of told you once and you thought I was fucking with you. I'm not from here. I'm from an alternate reality."

Isaac's brow furrowed. "Where you were about to be arrested for murder before popping into this world."

"That's right."

The look on his face conveyed deep exasperation. He believed she was still playing games with him and was close to getting genuinely angry about it. In a way, she couldn't blame him. Six months ago, she would've felt the same way if someone told her a similar story.

He leveled a forefinger at her. "But what—"

Allison never heard the rest of whatever he'd been about to say because that was when the metal door rattled up on its tracks, surprising both of them.

Isaac whirled about just in time to take a shotgun blast to the chest.

TWENTY-THREE

A SLENDER MIDDLE-AGED WOMAN with long, curly brown hair squinted at Allison over the barrel of the pump shotgun gripped in her hands. She wore a red flannel shirt open over a faded old Whitesnake T-shirt and jeans with ragged holes at the knees. The woman wasn't anyone she'd ever seen before this moment. Not back there at the Walmart or anywhere else.

She gestured at Allison with the barrel of the shotgun. "Get up out of that chair, girlie."

Allison rose shakily from the chair. "Please don't hurt me."

"Drop that knife."

Allison allowed the steak knife to slip from her fingers and land with a clatter on the cement floor. At the woman's direction, she kicked it under the nearest of the metal shelving units. She hated to lose the only weapon she had, but knew she wasn't actually surrendering much. A flimsy steak knife couldn't offer much in the way of real protection against a shotgun. Unless she was able to get in close, that is, and jab the blade into her throat, but the likelihood of that happening was right around nil. This lady didn't strike her as the sort to let her guard down enough to make herself vulnerable.

Another gesture with the barrel of the shotgun. "Come toward me until I tell you to stop."

A gurgling sound from the floor made Allison look down. Isaac was still alive, but the amount of blood gushing from the hole in his chest made it clear he wasn't long for this world. She was no medical professional, but she was sure he didn't have more than a minute or two left. He raised a shaky hand and reached for her as she stepped by him, but she ignored this. There was nothing she could do for him and she didn't actually care to help him anyway. He was at death's door and for all she knew she might soon follow him into the abyss. She wondered if he'd had some conflict with this unknown woman, one that culminated in this deadly attack. Perhaps she was another victim of his predatory inclinations, someone he'd taken advantage of in a vulnerable moment. That seemed like a decent guess, but that's all it was.

"Stop right there."

The woman's tone was stern, brooking no back talk.

Allison stopped moving forward and stood as still as a statue, scarcely daring to breathe as she awaited the older woman's next instruction. She'd seen for herself the brutally destructive power of the shotgun and felt close to crumbling under the mental pressure of its barrel aimed at her chest.

"Turn around and drop to your knees."

Allison sniffled and did as she'd been told, whimpering when her bare knees touched the cold cement floor. At that point, she fully expected to soon feel the muzzle of the shotgun pressing against the back of her head. For the third time within recent hours she found herself seemingly moments away from death and oblivion. It wasn't an experience that became more pleasant with repetition.

The woman moved closer.

"Put your hands behind your back."

Allison didn't want to do it, but what choice did she have?

As soon as her hands were behind her back, the woman dropped to her knees behind her. She sensed the shotgun was no longer aimed directly at her and for a moment entertained the idea of attempting an impression of an action movie heroine. In her head, she saw herself whirling about and kicking the weapon out of the woman's hands, then fighting against her in a desperate struggle to retrieve it.

But nothing like that happened.

She remained still as the woman cinched a zip tie tightly into place around her wrists. The hard plastic bit into her skin. Five feet directly in front of her, Isaac was no longer struggling against the inevitable. He was gone, his chest no longer rising and falling in a futile effort to draw in more labored breaths. She felt no grief at his loss, nor any horror at the violent manner of his death. This was a man who thought nothing of cheating on his beautiful wife with some random highway skank. It could reasonably be argued he'd gotten nothing less than exactly what he deserved. Allison was concerned only with whatever was coming next.

"Please don't hurt me," she said again.

The woman put her mouth against Allison's ear. "I'm locking you in here for a bit, girlie, so you best get comfortable. Got some stuff that needs taking care of before I deal with you. Keep your mouth shut and don't call out for help. I run this place and trust me when I say I'll know if you start acting up." She seized a handful of Allison's hair and gave it a savage twist that caused some strands to pull free of her scalp. "You gonna behave?"

Allison sniffled. "Y-yes."

The woman's mouth pressed against Allison's ear again, her teeth nipping at her earlobe. "See that you do."

She planted a palm flat against the middle of her back and gave her a hard shove forward. With her hands bound behind her back, she was unable to brace herself. She cried out as her face smacked against the hard, cold floor, the sound eliciting a chuckle from her captor.

The woman got to her feet and moved away from Allison.

"You belong to me now, girl. And I'm never gonna let you go."

The overhead fluorescent bulbs winked out as she hit the light switch. Moments later, the heavy metal door rattled down on its tracks and clanged shut, enveloping Allison in darkness.

TWENTY-FOUR

TIME PASSED SLOWLY IN THE darkness. The woman didn't return until several hours later, so that was part of it, but Allison's helplessness enhanced the perception of aching, almost unbearable slowness.

Allison began to feel uncomfortable in her face-down position and rolled onto her side, but the change didn't much reduce her level of discomfort. Before long, this new position became more uncomfortable than the previous one, so she flopped onto her stomach again, whining in misery. She changed position a few more times after that and each time the constraint of her arms contributed to steadily worsening muscular aches. She moaned and cried out in frustration and tried contorting her body in a way that would allow her to slip her bound wrists over her ass and legs and then bring them to the front of her body. The effort failed due to the utter lack of give in the strip of hard plastic. Bound in regular handcuffs, she might have been able to do it, but not like this.

She couldn't see Isaac in the dark, but she knew the approximate location of his corpse. An idea came to her, one she would've been disgusted by once upon a time, but that was back in the days before she started experimenting in corpse mutilation and cannibalism.

After waddling over to the dead man on her knees, she draped herself over his midsection, using him like a pillow. His shirt was sticky with blood, but that didn't bother her, nor did the slight wheeze of air that came out of the hole in his chest when her weight fell atop him. The physical relief she felt was immediate and significant, so much so that she wound up shifting around some more so she could lie intertwined with him like a lover, with her face pressed into the crook of his neck.

This period of physical relief allowed her mind to turn to contemplation of other things, such as trying to imagine how she might extricate herself, once again, from a seemingly hopeless situation. She tried summoning The Visitor, but he didn't respond. The low-level connection she always felt even when the entity wasn't physically in her presence was gone, completely severed as far as she could tell. Its absence filled her with despair. She again had that sense of being punished or taught a lesson, though a faint part of her persisted in clinging to the hope this was a temporary state of affairs and not a permanent case of abandonment. The latter would mean doom and she didn't want that, despite her brief flirtation with suicide earlier.

Variations of these same thoughts continued to whirl about in her head in a maddeningly circular way, taking her nowhere, offering no solutions or enlightenment of any kind. Even small epiphanies proved elusive. The protracted period of confinement dragged on for so long she began to think it might last forever. Logic suggested otherwise. The storage unit was a crime scene in need of scrubbing, for one thing. Isaac's killer would have to get rid of the body if she didn't want to go to jail. In this case, however, exhaustion and paranoia soon superseded logic, turning her perception of time elastic. A short stretch of minutes felt like hours. Actual hours felt like days and weeks.

After an indeterminate number of hours, her racing thoughts at last began to slow down. A state of near delirium became inevitable. She snuggled in against Isaac as she would with a real lover—minus the ability to embrace him, of course—and engaged in conversation with him.

There was a degree of self-awareness at the outset of this interlude. She knew she was the one voicing his replies to her questions and speculative ruminations, but after a while the line between reality and imagination began to blur. Awareness of her mouth moving during his responses faded and his voice became what she heard rather than her own. He said sensitive and reassuring things, revealing a depth she hadn't imagined he possessed. She became mildly aroused and started kissing his cooling flesh. On the neck and then on the mouth, sliding her tongue between his blood-flecked lips.

She was still doing this when the storage unit's door rattled upwards on its tracks again. The overhead lights flickered on, making Allison blink rapidly for a few moments, her eyes needing time to adjust after so long a period in the dark.

Isaac's killer snorted laughter. "Well, ain't this sweet."

Allison slowly turned her head toward the woman.

She was still armed, but had traded the shotgun for a pistol. Her outfit was different, too, consisting of black leggings and a zipped-up black hoodie over a shirt she couldn't see. She looked like a movie assassin dressed up to carry out a hit. Beyond her, parked on the strip of pavement between rows of storage units was a beige pickup truck, an older model with rust spots. It was nighttime outside now. There was no sign of the Lexus.

"I thought you were never coming back."

The woman laughed again, a sound laced with palpable cruelty. "Aw. Did you miss me?"

Allison sniffled and gave one weak shake of her head.

The woman approached her, bent down, and grabbed her by the crook of an arm. "Time for you to get up. You and me are going for a ride."

She roughly hauled Allison to her feet and steered her toward the open door.

"I don't want to go anywhere with you."

The woman smacked the back of her head, making her stumble. "Well, tough shit. You ain't got any say in it."

Allison walked out of the storage unit and, at her captor's direction, approached the rear of the truck, where the tailgate was hanging open. A tie-down tarp was stretched out over the truck bed. She knew right away she was meant to crawl in under it, but didn't see how she could do so with the zip tie around her wrists. Taking a desperate look around, she saw no other vehicles in this section of the facility. All the other unit doors were closed and locked.

The woman pulled down the door to Isaac's unit and clicked the padlock back into place.

She chuckled. "You can scream if you want. We're the only ones here now. I made sure of that."

"Why are you doing this?"

The woman approached Allison from behind, pressing the muzzle of the pistol against her side. "Honey, you're better off not fretting over that. It's just one of those things in life you can't really explain. I saw you on the security camera when you came in with your boyfriend and knew I had to have you. Like, I couldn't let you leave here without taking you from him."

Allison's hands clenched into fists, a need for violence rising and coiling within her, her inability to act on the impulse making her nostrils flare. "You talk about me like I'm an object, but I'm a person. You have no right to do this."

She was aware of the inherent hypocrisy of these words as she uttered them, knowing she was guilty of far worse than this. The knowledge, however, in no way dampened her anger. Things like this were only wrong when done by ordinary people like this redneck, gun-toting mega-cunt. Allison was *not* ordinary. She was special and extreme allowances must always be made for special people. The Visitor selecting her as a host for his parasitical needs was proof of her specialness. His absence in no way negated that.

The woman wedged the muzzle of the gun harder against her side. "Bitch, I can do whatever I want and ain't nobody gonna stop me. I'm gonna help you up into the truck now. Make any funny moves and I'll put a bullet in you."

Allison surprised herself with a soft laugh. "You wouldn't do that. You want me alive, not dead. Let me ride up front with you. I promise I won't do anything stupid."

A silent moment passed, during which the woman seemed to seriously contemplate the notion.

Then she sighed. "Nah. Wouldn't want anyone seeing you and me together once we're out of here. You're getting under that tarp. *Now*."

She rapped the butt of the pistol against the back of Allison's head for further emphasis. The resulting pain was like a blade through her skull. After that, she accepted this part of the battle as lost and opted not to fight the woman when she worked to heft her up over the open tailgate. The woman then prodded her with the gun, getting her to squirm further into the truck bed.

She smirked as she peered in at Allison. "No screaming or crying out for help. You do anything like that and I'll break every bone in your body with a baseball bat. Don't believe me?"

Allison whined a little and said, "I believe you'll hurt me, yes."

The woman chuckled. "Get ready for a bumpy ride. I live out in the country and you're gonna get tossed around some. Think of it like a roller coaster ride without a safety bar."

She laughed nastily one more time.

Then she slammed the tailgate shut.

Minutes later, they were riding away from the storage facility and out to the countryside.

TWENTY-FIVE

THE RIDE OUT TO THE woman's isolated country home was as bumpy as promised. By the time it came to a merciful conclusion, Allison felt like she'd been tossed around inside a giant tin can. The truck came to a stop following a period of crunching over gravel, its engine continuing to rumble a few moments longer before dying with a rattling sputter. A moment later Allison heard a squeal of rusty hinges as her captor got out of the truck. Booted feet hit the ground and the door was thrown shut.

Shortly thereafter, the tailgate came open with another squeal of old hinges. The woman reached in and grabbed her by the ankles with both hands, neither of which currently had a gun in them. She had mere seconds to consider whether this might be her last feasible chance to fight back, which wasn't nearly enough time to adequately weigh the pros and cons of the matter. The woman grunted in exertion as she pulled her out from under the tarp. She kept at it until Allison's waist was at the edge of the tailgate, with her bare legs dangling in the cool air. At that point, she grabbed the back of her shorts and hauled her the rest of the way out. She hit the ground on her feet and wobbled a little, but managed to stay upright.

A voice rang out from somewhere nearby. "Who the hell is that?"

Allison turned her head and saw a young girl standing on the long porch of the dilapidated old country house. She was pretty in a trashy way, with big breasts and long blonde hair. The blonde came from a bottle, as evidenced by the prominent dark roots. She wore only a lacy black bra and denim cutoffs so small they were no bigger than a bikini bottom. Standing barefoot on the porch with a cigarette burning between two pinched fingers, she watched the unfolding drama with only mild interest. The door to the house was standing open. A television tuned to some obnoxious reality show blared from somewhere inside.

The girl looked like a slightly thicker and much younger version of the woman who'd taken her.

Mother and daughter, probably.

The mother said, "She's my new pet. Go fetch that old muzzle, will ya. I'm gonna take her around back."

The younger one stared hard at Allison for a moment. "Where did you find her?"

"At work. Don't worry. Nobody saw me with her." She laughed in an insidious way. "Nobody still alive, that is."

The girl frowned. "You killed somebody at work?"

"Like I said, don't worry about it. I've got your brothers taking care of the cleanup and shit."

The girl rolled her eyes and took a puff on her cigarette. "So that's where those idiots went off to in a hurry. They wouldn't tell me shit."

The mother snickered. "Because they're good boys who do what their mama tells them without any back talk. You got no need to know anything unless I say so. Now go fetch that goddamn muzzle and meet me out back."

The girl sneered. "Whatever."

She turned away from them and went back into the house, slamming the door shut behind her.

The mother heaved an irritated sigh. "Kids. They're a treasure, but sometimes they can make you wanna slap the shit out of them. You know what I mean?"

Allison shook her head. "I wouldn't know. I don't have any."

The gun pressed into her side again. There went her hope of the weapon no longer being part of the equation. The woman must have stowed it in a pocket of her hoodie while dragging her out of the truck bed.

"This way." She grabbed Allison by a shoulder and turned her so she was facing a corner of the house. "We're going around back. Get moving."

She gave her a push in the back.

Allison again stumbled forward but managed to stay on her feet. A second push, however, sent her to her knees. The woman's subsequent cackle was tinged with sadistic glee. Allison yearned for free hands and the fighting skills of a ninja. Beating this bitch to a bloody pulp would feel so glorious after all the rough treatment. Borderline orgasmic, even. It was an alluring fantasy, but it also angered her, because she knew transforming it into reality was impossible.

The woman hauled her to her feet and got her moving again.

As Allison stumbled forward, little dips in the uneven ground almost made her lose her footing several more times. There was some exterior lighting, but negotiating the unfamiliar terrain at night with her hands bound behind her back was nonetheless difficult.

The house sat in a clearing at the end of a private lane in a densely wooded area. Any other houses that might be nearby were hidden from view. For all Allison knew—having made the trip out here sealed up in darkness—it was possible these people lived miles away from their nearest neighbor. The pessimist in her strongly suspected this was the case, which meant her situation was even more hopeless than she already believed. In that event, she could scream for help at the top of her lungs for hours and hours without anyone ever coming to her rescue.

No fence enclosed the backyard, which was bordered instead by a ring of tall trees, the edge of the forest. The woods looked ominous in the dark, like a shadowy portal to a land of nightmares populated with twisted fairytale creatures. She dismissed the fanciful notion with a sneer, knowing beyond doubt that no creature of myth could be any scarier than her captor.

Another tree stood alone in the middle of the yard, a tall old one with a wide trunk, its roots partially visible above ground. Her captor gave her another nudge in the back and told her to head in that direction. Looped around the base of the tree was a rusty old chain. Attached to the end of it was a thick leather collar with spikes, the sight of which filled her with dread, because it was already obvious what the woman had in mind.

"Stop right there."

Allison stopped less than ten feet shy of the tree.

The collar was at her feet.

"On your knees."

Allison sniffled. "Please don't do this. I'll do anything you want. *Anything.* Just please don't chain me up like an animal."

"On your knees or I shoot you in the back."

Allison still didn't believe the woman would shoot her, at least not at this early stage of things. She hadn't gone to the trouble of killing a man and bringing her out here just to do that. The woman was clearly motivated by the same compulsion that forced her to flee the mob at Walmart. She wanted to possess her. The threats of violence were just to keep her in line, but this in no way meant she was safe from physical harm.

She dropped to her knees and tried not to descend into hysterical sobbing as the woman approached her from behind and put a hand on her shoulder. "Honey, you're gonna do anything I want because you don't have any other fucking choice. Pets have to obey. That's just the way it is."

She retrieved the collar from the ground and cinched it into place around Allison's neck, buckling it uncomfortably tight.

Allison grimaced, gasping for air.

The woman tapped the barrel of the pistol against the underside of her chin, prompting her to lift up her head. "That old collar looks good on you. Like you were born to wear it."

"It hurts."

The woman smiled. "Good."

A door opened at the back of the house and the daughter emerged from a rectangle of light to stand on the small stoop. She held up an object that was hard to see from this distance in the dark, but the mother waved to the girl, beckoning her down into the yard.

Despite the sharp chill in the air, the girl was still in immodest garb better suited to hanging out at a trailer park on a hot summer day. In her place, Allison would at least have thrown on a jacket. Up close, the tiny denim cutoffs looked one frayed thread away from falling off her body.

The mother backhanded Allison. "Stop ogling my daughter."

"I wasn't—"

"Shut up."

With a tilt of her chin, the woman gestured for the object gripped in her daughter's hand. "Hand that over. You never put it on right. Kept falling off that last bitch we had out here."

The girl handed the object to her mother with an annoyed huff. "Whatever. It's got too many fucking straps."

Allison's bulging eyes tracked the object as it passed between them. In basic appearance, it was similar to the restraint mask

Hannibal Lecter was made to wear in *Silence of the Lambs*, the main differences being a ball-gag attachment in place of the mouth guard and additional straps. Her heart raced at the thought of the gag being forced into her mouth. She was already having trouble breathing, thanks to the collar. Adding the gag to the mix might seal her fate. Her jaw trembled as the urge to say something grew stronger.

The woman handed the gun to her daughter. "Keep that aimed at her head while I get this thing on her."

The girl said nothing as she accepted the gun and moved back a few steps. Her expression remained impassive as her mother pressed the restraint mask against Allison's face and began fussing with the straps.

A process that stopped when the gunshot rang out.

TWENTY-SIX

THE LOUD CRACK OF THE gun's report made Allison scream. She waited to feel the delayed pain of a bullet entering her body, but it wasn't forthcoming. Another loud bang elicited a frightened squeal, but this time she saw the mother's body jerk and then stagger away from her. There was a look of stunned disbelief on the woman's face as she struggled to turn toward her daughter. She appeared on the verge of saying something, but the words went unspoken as the gun boomed again. This time a bullet punched through her forehead. She took another staggering backward step, dropped to her knees, and toppled over.

Allison looked at the woman's unblinking eyes.

She was dead.

With only one strap in place, the restraint mask fell away from her face and hung off her chin. Her heart felt like it wanted to jump out of her chest as her struggle to breathe neared a crisis point. She made gagging noises and felt her face grow hot.

The girl's placid demeanor stood in stark contrast to her own. There was no hint of distress anywhere in those pretty features as she walked over to her mother and stood over her. Her expression didn't change as she aimed the pistol at the unmoving woman's torso and fired three more bullets into her already dead flesh.

Allison cringed with each shot. Her ears were ringing and her head felt overpressurized, as if it might explode at any second. When the girl turned toward her with the faintest ghost of a smile touching the edges of her mouth, she would've screamed had she been capable of it. The girl's lips moved. She was saying something to Allison, but the ringing in her ears blotted out the words.

The girl came closer and raised her voice. "I said, I can't believe I did that."

Allison shivered and made another gagging sound, but this time the girl's words were audible.

And now she thought, *That makes two of us.*

The girl frowned. "Your face is turning red."

Allison tried to speak, but could only make more gagging sounds.

The girl stepped even closer. "Hold on and be still. I'm not gonna hurt you, I promise."

She reached behind Allison's head and undid the one strap keeping the restraint mask in place. After tearing it away and tossing it aside, she unbuckled the dog collar and removed it from Allison's neck.

"There. That better?"

Allison dragged in multiple ragged gasps of air and then went into a violent coughing fit that hurt her throat, making her feel like she was gargling with rusty razor blades. The girl rubbed her back in an apparent effort to soothe her and made noises of reassurance. Being treated so tenderly by someone who'd just blown away her own mother was beyond bizarre. It was easy to conclude the girl was just the latest link in a human chain of obsession, one that would continue to grow as long as she remained in this world. Just like her mother before her, she wanted to possess Allison, to have her all to herself.

The girl made a face as she listened to the ragged hacking sounds. "You want some water?"

Allison's teeth chattered as she nodded. "Y-yes."

The girl started moving toward the back of the house. "I'll get something to cut you out of that zip tie, too. Be right back."

After watching the girl disappear into the house, Allison got shakily to her feet and took a look around. The spooky dark line of trees encircling the house tempted her. She could run into that darkness and disappear easily enough, but what made her hesitate was not knowing how large this wooded area was. If it was too big, she might never find her way out again. Even with her hands free, it would be dangerous. With the zip tie still in place, odds were good she wouldn't be seen again until some hunter stumbled upon her desiccated corpse months later.

She glanced at the woman on the ground. Isaac's killer, dead now herself. The keys to her pickup truck might be somewhere in that black hoodie. As Allison's coughing fit at last began to subside, she couldn't help laughing at the direction of her thoughts. So what if the woman's keys were in one of those puffy pockets? Even if she could snag them, she wouldn't be able to drive that old rust bucket of a truck with her hands tied behind her back.

The only other option she could think of was to run back around to the front of the house and keep on running down that private lane until she reached an actual road. At which point . . . what? Was she supposed to hope for someone else to come along and pick her up? In her current semi-helpless state, that didn't seem like a good idea. There was a strong likelihood anyone who picked her up would fall victim to the same compulsion to possess.

She supposed there was a slim chance that might not happen. Not *everyone* who set eyes on her at Walmart joined that mob, after all. Some didn't even give her a second glance. But the percentage of people who did was high enough to warrant deep concern. For whatever reason, *those* people were more attuned to her essential alienness. The maddening thing was there was no way she could tell the difference between the obsessed and the non-obsessed until she was either in their clutches or running for her life.

She was still debating it all when the back door to the house came open again and the girl stepped out onto the stoop. That was it, then. Her chance to flee had fled. She could only hope the daughter wouldn't harm her in any permanent way before she could figure out some other means of getting free.

The girl had a strange bounce to her gait as she descended the steps and started across the patchy lawn. Any more bounce to it and she'd be skipping like a schoolgirl. She was smiling again, too. Beaming, really. Allison was again struck by the incongruity of her sunny demeanor and the cold-blooded murder she'd just committed.

The girl came bearing the things she'd promised, a plastic bottle of water and a kitchen knife. She laughed as she neared Allison. "You look so fucking confused."

No point denying it.

Allison shrugged. "You could say that."

Some of the happy glow faded from the girl's features. "That bitch made my life miserable for a long time. She was more pimp than mother, if you know what I mean."

Allison frowned. "Um . . ."

"Whatever that makes you think, the truth is even worse," the girl elaborated, the bright smile disappearing completely now. "She kept me under tight control for a long time and never made a single mistake." Now the smile flickered back to life. "Until she handed me that gun."

Allison didn't know what to say to that, so only nodded.

The girl stepped behind her and used the knife to saw through the zip tie. "There ya go. That's got to feel better, right? She used those on me sometimes, if I wasn't behaving right. She'd zip me up and stick me in a closet overnight. Or worse."

Allison cleared her throat and found her voice. "That sounds . . . terrible."

She ignored the sneering inner voice accusing her of hypocrisy again.

The girl moved back into view and handed Allison the water bottle. "But none of that shit's the real reason I did what I did."

Allison screwed the cap off the bottle and let it fall to the ground. She drank greedily, not caring as some of the water sluiced down over her chin. By the time she took the bottle away from her mouth, she'd consumed two-thirds of its contents. She heaved a satisfied breath and said, "So what's the real reason?"

The girl gave a strangely excited squeal as she jumped up and down a couple times. "Come on, you know why! I recognized you as soon as I saw you."

Allison tilted her head, narrowing her eyes in suspicion. "You did?"

The first thing she thought of was her crimes back in Ohio. A lot of hours had passed now since those cops came to her house, maybe enough for the news to start getting out. Then she felt like smacking herself for even thinking that. Those things had happened in another reality. She hadn't killed anyone in this world. Yet.

So what the hell?

The girl rolled her eyes. "Of course I fucking did. You're Allie Cook!"

This time Allison's head tilted so far to one side it felt in danger of falling off her shoulders.

Her mouth opened, but no words emerged.

What the fuck?

The girl's amusement showed no signs of abating. Once again, Allison felt nearly overcome with a sense of the surreal, only this time it went much deeper. She felt on the verge of being irretrievably sucked into a whirlpool of mind-bending mystery. The girl wasn't lying about having recognized her. She no longer harbored any doubt on that count. No one had called her Allie since early childhood, but there was no denying it was a version of her name. Hearing it emerge from the mouth of this absolute stranger in this strange land made her feel slightly dizzy. Adding to the sense of strangeness was the way she'd uttered it with such unmistakable reverence.

The girl gave another of those excited squeals and jumped into the air one more time. "I just can't fucking believe it! The director of *The Doomed Ones* in *my* backyard. The modern queen of horror. That's, like, my favorite fucking movie of all goddamn time. This is fucking crazy."

A light popped on in Allison's head.

A sense of dumbfounded astonishment engulfed her as her mind rewound to months ago, when The Visitor left her a movie by that same name with a stack of other ones. Those other movies were requests. At the time the unfamiliar movie's inclusion with the others struck her as a case of The Visitor fucking with her for no apparent reason. As it turned out, there was a method to the madness.

Should've fucking known better.

Now she couldn't believe she'd filed the thing away after barely glancing at it.

The girl's smile slowly morphed into a look of confusion. "But what are you doing out here in the middle of redneck country? I thought you were filming a new movie in California with Ryan Laettner."

Allison wanted this girl to go on thinking she was this world's Allison Cook for a while longer, but she didn't yet trust herself to formulate a lie that would believably explain an apparently famous filmmaker's presence here, in this unlikely place, in this even unlikelier situation.

She settled for saying, "You know a lot about me, but I don't know anything about you. What's your name?"

The girl's smile returned. "Jazlyn. But you can call me Jazz. Everyone does."

"Why I'm here is a long story. Tell me something, Jazz. You got any beer in that house?"

Jazz groaned. "There's loads of beer. Mom and my brothers are terrible drunks. Well, mom *was*." She giggled. "She's not anything anymore, is she?"

Allison thought, *Wow.*

She shrugged. "Guess not."

Jazz laughed. "You can help yourself to as much of their beer as you want, but first can you help me drag this dead sack of shit into the woods? I don't want my brothers seeing her when they get back from whatever the fuck they're doing."

There wasn't much Allison wouldn't do for an ice-cold beer at this point.

She nodded. "Let's get to draggin'."

TWENTY-SEVEN

AFTER HIDING THE CORPSE AWAY in some brush some twenty feet into the woods, Allison followed Jazz back to the yard and then across the lawn to the house. They passed within range of the discarded dog collar and for a moment she was torn between an urge to kick the collar away in a show of contempt or grab the chain and wrap it around her savior's neck. The girl wouldn't see it coming. She was in the presence of her idol, or so she believed, whose life she'd probably just saved. It'd be easy to quickly pull the chain tight and ride her to the ground, holding her down while she struggled beneath her and choked to death.

The idea tempted her strongly. She wouldn't have to come up with a story to explain why she was here in Tennessee being kidnapped instead of directing a film in California. The biggest reason to avoid that was it was a lie she'd have to keep perpetuating and expanding upon as long as she was around this girl. Just thinking about that was exhausting. Also, violence and murder was becoming a thing she actually enjoyed. So long as she wasn't on the receiving end of it, of course. The prospect of feeling Jazz struggle and perish beneath her excited her. No point denying it.

That excitement was complicated by a dawning awareness that she actually liked the girl. They had a burgeoning natural rapport, which was something Allison hadn't experienced with anyone since her friends died. There was zero chance of them maintaining an ongoing friendship beyond this night, of course. The mother's murder couldn't be hidden forever and there were other people who lived in this house. Hiding out here long-term wasn't an option. And at some point Jazz would realize the Allie Cook she'd saved wasn't the one she idolized. She would have to be gone before that happened, but maybe for a short while she could pretend to have a real friend again.

Allison lagged a few feet behind Jazz as they neared the house. The dog collar and chain were behind her now, but her eyes kept going to the gun tucked away in the waistband of the girl's denim shorts at the small of her back. Snatching it away from her would be even easier than what she'd previously considered. Once again, she opted against acting on the impulse.

Instead she followed Jazz up the stairs to the stoop and then into a dingy kitchen. The white linoleum floor looked like it hadn't been mopped in many months, maybe years. Dirty dishes were stacked high in the sink, from which wafted a smell of rotting food.

Jazz looked embarrassed. "I'm sorry. I know you're used to staying in nicer places."

Allison thought of the shoddy current state of her own house back in Ohio and tried not to laugh. It wasn't easy. She glanced at the refrigerator and looked at Jazz. "Help myself, right?"

Jazz nodded. "Yeah, absolutely. Only thing is . . ." She frowned as she trailed off. "But, well, this is embarrassing . . . but . . ."

"Spit it out."

Jazz shifted her weight from one leg to the other, showing her nervousness. "I thought you were a recovering alcoholic. You talk about it in a lot of the interviews, especially in that one in *Rue Morgue* last summer."

Some silent moments went by as Allison digested this information and tried to think of a way to incorporate it in whatever story she was about to tell this girl.

She sighed. "I'm the one who should be embarrassed. I know a lot of my fans look up to me for that, but I fell off the wagon a few days ago and sort of went on an epic bender. Things got a little out of control. To tell you the truth, I'm not even sure how I wound up in Tennessee." She tried arranging her features in a way that showed regret. "I'm sorry if I've let you down, Jazz."

Allison again tried not to laugh.

The story was perfect, giving her a vague form of blanket cover that could at least partly explain away any inconsistencies in whatever else she told this girl. Until, of course, this world's Allison Cook decided to do something annoying, like posting updates on social media contradicting what she was saying.

Jazz surprised her by pulling her into a hug. "You haven't let me down, Allie. You're an amazing person, but you're still human, right? I'd never judge you for something like that. I know you'll come back from this stronger than ever."

Allison's chin was on the girl's shoulder.

She looked down at the gun and thought again about grabbing it.

The urge was stronger this time.

But then Jazz eased out of the embrace and clasped hands with her. "Come with me a minute. I want to show you something in my room."

Allison glanced back at the refrigerator with a strong pang of regret, but allowed herself to be dragged out of the kitchen. They passed into a dumpy living room that looked trapped in time, a relic of the 1970s. Lots of wood paneling and chintzy adornments on the wall. An orange sofa and green shag carpeting so filthy setting it on fire would be a better option than ever attempting to clean it. A Zenith floor-model TV like the one she had back home would've rounded out the retro decor nicely, but a modern flatscreen model was mounted on the wall opposite the hideous ancient sofa instead. A reality show featuring scantily clad, beautiful young people was playing on the screen, presumably the same one Jazlyn was watching when she came out on the front porch earlier. The sound was muted now, sparing Allison from having to hear any more of the cast's vapid bickering.

Jazz led her down a hallway with the same puke-green shag carpeting on the floor, moving past multiple rooms with closed doors until they arrived at another one near the end of the hallway. This room's door was also closed but wasn't pulled all the way into the frame.

The girl pushed the door open and they entered what was obviously her own bedroom. Against the wall to their left as they passed through the door was a long dresser with a bookcase on top of it, the shelves of which were crowded with an assortment of movies and books about movies. Every inch of wall space was covered with posters and glossy pictures clipped from magazines. The posters were mostly theatrical posters for horror movies, but a few were of horror media personalities. One from the latter category showed Darcy the mail girl from *The Last Drive-In* in a revealing low-cut top, pretending to lick blood from the edge of a knife. Another one showed Elvira lounging in lingerie against a spooky background. And, right above the headboard of Jazlyn's bed, was a poster of Allie Cook.

The image showed the filmmaker decked out in black leather pants and stiletto heel boots. She was topless, her torso spattered with fake blood, her breasts mostly hidden by the way she was posed, with a big axe gripped in her hands and held at chest level. At her feet was the body of some pretend victim. The model playing dead was flat on his stomach, with his head turned away from the camera. The director stood with one of her heels on his back. Her expression was sneering and playful at the same time.

"That one's my favorite. I ordered it from your website last year."

Allison's mouth was hanging open.

She closed it before turning toward the sound of the girl's voice. "Oh, yeah?"

Jazz was over by her dresser now, sorting through her movies and books. "Sure did. Paid extra to have it signed. Kind of expensive for a poster, but totally worth it."

Allison's attention returned to the poster of Allie Cook. This time she got closer to the bed and leaned over the mattress for a better look. Sure enough, in the bottom right-hand corner was a scrawled signature, one that looked eerily close to her own handwriting. Beneath the signature was an inscription that read, *Queen of Horror*.

She couldn't help shaking her head in stunned wonder. A wave of emotion surprised her, making her eyes glimmer with tears. She and the woman on the poster looked alike, but they weren't the same, not even close. The Allie Cook of this world was a titanic success, a revered creative artist with the world at her feet, as symbolically represented in the poster. She was confident, powerful, sexy, and happy.

Whereas she, a sad sack copy of that vibrant woman, was none of those things. No one in her own world idolized Allison Cook. Why would they? She was a nobody, a failure whose own bigger ambitions would forever go unrealized. In truth, she'd allowed them to wither on the vine years and years ago, written off as unrealistic. She thought again of that last moment in her world, standing in front of the mirror with the knife to her throat. Now she fervently wished she could return to that moment and go through with it, feel the blade cut deep and release the useless life-blood imprisoned in her veins.

"Allie?"

She heard a snapping of fingers somewhere near her head. The sound made her flinch slightly. She wiped moisture from her eyes and turned toward Jazz again. "Sorry. Got sort of lost in space there for a minute."

Jazz frowned. "Are you okay?"

Allison sniffled and wiped away more tears, laughing to cover her embarrassment. "Yeah. I'm fine." She let out a big breath and forced a smile. "I guess sometimes I kind of lose sight of how much I mean to my fans. It's easy to get caught up in the fame and success and forget about them. Then something like this happens and it almost feels like a message from above. Like a wake-up call. You know what I mean?"

She couldn't believe the load of unadulterated horseshit spewing from her mouth.

Jazz, however, was nodding along as she listened to it all. The look on her face was one of pure, worshipful rapture. "Oh, I totally get it. Like, I love you so fucking much, and I never expected to be in the same room with you. Never in a million, billion years. It feels like destiny."

"Totally." Allison's smile faded as she took note of the items gripped in the girl's hands. "What's all that?"

The girl's expression turned sheepish. "These are your movies. All the ones I have, anyway. I was wondering if you could sign them for me. I'm sorry to ask. I know this is a fucked-up time for you right now, but I might never get another chance and I'd be pissed at myself later for letting it slip away."

Allison summoned her smile back and accepted the tall stack of DVDs and Blu-rays. It was around a dozen movies in all, more than she would've expected, which could only mean Allie Cook had been a working filmmaker from a young age. Once again, she felt a deep amazement tinged with more than a little bitter jealousy. "Of course I'll sign them for you. Got a pen?"

TWENTY-EIGHT

THE GIRL DASHED OUT OF the room, presumably to retrieve a pen from elsewhere in the house. While awaiting her return, Allison sat on the edge of the bed and sorted through the stack of movies. An explanation for the large number of films soon presented itself.

Allie Cook started off as an actress, it seemed, one who appeared in a lot of movies in a short period of time early in her career. Then came an apparent transition to working primarily behind the camera, though she continued to act some as well. Even more impressively, she appeared to have sole screenwriting credit on *all* her directorial efforts. Allison's bitterness continued to grow in direct proportion to her burgeoning admiration for Allie Cook.

She shook her head.

I sort of hate you, you impressive bitch.

Then she arrived at the bottom of the stack and saw *The Doomed Ones*. As soon as her fingers touched the blue case, she felt something shift inside her head, a familiar intrusion that nearly made her weep with joy. The hair at the nape of her neck prickled and gooseflesh dotted her arms. She shivered in pleasure as the unnatural chill enveloped her.

The Visitor.

More tears in her eyes.

I thought you were gone forever. Please don't ever leave me again.

She brushed the front of the Blu-ray case with her fingertips, feeling the chill deepen. A few minutes ago, she was spouting bullshit about signs from above to the fangirl, but this felt like a real one. It couldn't just be coincidence that the entity chose this moment to reestablish rudimentary contact. Nothing specific was being communicated yet, but she wasn't concerned about that. The Visitor wouldn't return without good reason. There was a purpose here, she was sure of it. A design of some kind. There probably had been all along. How else to explain being saved by a superfan of her doppelganger in this world? The odds of that just randomly happening had to be astronomical.

No.

There was a bigger picture here. Something intensely meaningful. She just needed to figure out what that was.

After studying the ghostly images of the three young women on the Blu-ray's cover, she realized there was something familiar about them. Not that she actually recognized the young actresses pictured, but that sense of nagging familiarity wouldn't go away. A deep furrow creased the middle of her brow as she stared hard at the image and thought about it. Then it hit her out of nowhere, a lightning bolt of insight from the ether.

That's us.

Cassie, Julia, and me.

What the actual goddamn fuck?

Crazy as it seemed, there was no denying what her brain was telling her. It was right there in the styling of the hair, in the facial types. She flipped the case over and began to read the description on the back. In the same instant, she heard footsteps come racing down the hallway. Jazz on her way back, no doubt, moments from reentering the room.

Allie Cook wrote and directed *The Doomed Ones*, but did not star in it. The story was about three women, close friends, who obsess over a rare book of arcane magic. They turn against each other and tragedy ensues. It wasn't *exactly* the story of Allison and her friends, but it was close enough.

Jazz came bounding through the door, overcome with excitement once again. She handed Allison a Sharpie and sat next to her on the edge of the bed after setting the gun on her nightstand. Leaning close, she looked at the back of the Blu-ray case, her face lighting up when she recognized it. "Oh my God, I wish we could watch that one together." Her lower lip pooched out in a pout. "But you probably won't want to stay much longer, huh?"

Allison looked at her. "I mean, that's kind of up to you, isn't it? I'm not here by choice, remember. Your mother kidnapped me. And you've still got that gun. Am I free to go?"

A shocked expression replaced the girl's pout. "Of course you are. What do you think I am? I'm not like my mother. I'd never dream of hurting you or making you do anything you don't want. Jesus."

Hearing the hurt tone in the girl's voice twinged her remaining vestige of a conscience.

Allison sighed. "I've been through a lot just recently. I had to ask. I didn't mean to hurt your feelings." She craned her head around and glanced briefly at the poster above the headboard. "Do you think your mother recognized me? Any chance that's why she took me? As, like, a present for you?"

Jazz laughed. "I don't know if she recognized you. I mean, maybe. But even if she did, she definitely didn't do it for me. You heard what she said. You were gonna be *her* new pet."

Allison's brow furrowed again. "Whatever that means."

Jazz grimaced. "You don't want to know, trust me. Basically I just saved you from a real-life version of a backwoods horror movie."

Allison shuddered. "Doesn't sound like fun."

"It's not."

Allison removed the cap from the silver Sharpie and began the process of signing the movie cases. With some of the Blu-rays, she removed the cover insert and signed that instead. That was usually how it was done at horror cons where she met actors and filmmakers. At first it felt weird playing celebrity and pretending to be this cooler and far more accomplished version of herself, but there was nothing malicious in this particular deception. She was merely reacting to things as they happened and taking whatever steps seemed necessary to protect herself, and right now that meant allowing Jazlyn to continue buying into this case of mistaken identity.

The girl's giddiness was palpable as she sorted through the movies, admiring the newly acquired signatures. "Wow. Just wow. This is beyond fucking awesome. Thank you so much."

"No problem," Allison said, striving for a humble tone. "I like making my fans happy."

After getting up for a moment to set the stack of movies on her dresser, Jazz rejoined her on the edge of the mattress. She sat much closer this time and turned slightly toward her. "Speaking of making me happy." She put a hand on Allison's leg, just above the knee. "I know you're happily married and all, but I was thinking maybe there's another way you could thank me for saving you tonight." She leaned closer still, nuzzling her neck. "Your wife would never have to know."

Allison frowned.

My what?

Jazz kissed the side of her face, close to her ear. Her hand moved higher up the inside of her leg. "God, it'd be so amazing to fuck you after fantasizing about you for years."

Another kiss, this one on her cheek.

Back home, she would have fended off similar advances from any woman by now. She wasn't inclined that way and her rejections on the few occasions when things like this had happened were always swift and automatic. The only reason she hadn't done so yet in this case was because she was still so stunned by the casually dropped information bomb.

This world's version of Allison Cook was *married*.

To a *woman*.

What the fuck?

She felt in dire need of more information, but before she could ask for it, Jazz rose up from the edge of the mattress, gripped her by the waist, and heaved her backward. Allison fell upon the bed and saw Jazz looming over her, smiling as she removed her bra. She cast the garment aside and crawled up on the bed, her heavy breasts touching Allison's chest as she positioned herself above her. Before anything else happened, there was a prolonged moment of silent eye contact, giving her more than enough time to proclaim her lack of interest. The words were there, right at the edge of her tongue, but she didn't speak them.

Jazz kissed her.

Allison allowed her to do it, even kissing her back after a few moments, her hands going to the other girl's ass as her weight settled more heavily atop her. On a disconnected level, a part of her persisted in believing she was just playing along, waiting for the right moment to extricate herself from this situation before it went too far. The longer it went on, however, the less any part of her could go on believing that. She was becoming powerfully aroused and was close to not giving a damn how little sense this interlude made in context with the rest of her life. On more than one occasion as it was happening, she caught glimpses of the poster of her doppelganger, which triggered moments of feeling like she was having an out-of-body experience. She felt like Allie Cook watching Allison Cook pretend to be Allie Cook while deceptively exploiting the admiration of a fan.

It was weird as fuck.

Then she flinched at the sound of a loud bang from elsewhere in the house. An instant later, she realized what she'd heard was someone kicking in a door. It was followed by another jarringly loud sound. Someone out in the living room was yelling and stomping around.

Every trace of passion drained from Jazz's face. "Shit. My brothers are home."

TWENTY-NINE

THE PERSON WHO'D ENTERED THE house so noisily continued making a racket, stomping from room to room and calling out for his mother. Seconds later, a big man in a trucker hat came bursting into Jazlyn's room. He was clad in dirty jeans, a Kid Rock T-shirt strained by an enormous beer belly, and redneck shitkicker boots. A beard only partly obscured a face turned red by fury.

"What's going on in here, bitch? Where's Ma?"

Jazz rolled away from Allison with a groan of annoyance. "Goddammit, Wyatt. Can't you see I'm in the middle of something?"

Her brother scowled menacingly as he moved further into the room. "Yeah, right in the middle of breaking Ma's rules again. She's gonna tan your hide when I tell her I caught you doing dyke shit again. She might even stick you in the hole this time."

Allison looked at Jazz, her expression a perplexed one. "The hole?"

The girl scowled. "A pine box buried in the yard out back. Ma puts me in it sometimes when I've been extra bad."

Allison frowned. "That's fucked up."

Wyatt sneered as he undid his large rebel flag belt buckle and began to tug the belt free. "What's fucked up is you dirty bitches sinning under my sweet Ma's roof. I know she'd want you punished right away, so we'd best get on with it."

Jazz sat up straighter in the bed. The look on her face showed wariness but no actual fear yet. "What do you think you're gonna do with that thing?"

He snapped the belt against the dresser, making both women flinch. "I'm gonna whip you both until you're bloody." His face twisted in a look of savage, perverse amusement as he grabbed his crotch. "Then I might do some other things. Those are some nice titties, sis."

Jazz grunted. "No shit. Where's Austin?"

Her brother still had a hand on his crotch and was squeezing it as he continued to ogle his sister's exposed breasts. "Out back looking for Ma. There's fresh blood out there by the tree and Ma's truck is out front with the keys still in it. You know anything about any of that?"

Jazz stared at him without saying anything for a moment.

Then she made a grab for the gun.

Her brother snapped the belt at her hand, making her yelp in pain as leather lashed skin. The gun slid off the nightstand to the floor. Wyatt was bending over to snatch it up when Allison scrambled around on the bed and launched herself at him. She slammed into him and locked her limbs around him as he staggered backward and collided with the dresser. The impact caused some of the movies and books to slide off the shelves and rain down on their heads.

Wyatt pushed away from the dresser and tried shaking her loose, but Allison wouldn't allow it, clinging to him with a tenacity fueled in equal parts by fear and a reawakened thirst for violence. For a brief time, while pretending to be someone she wasn't, she felt almost normal, but that time was gone. It'd only been an illusion, anyway. This was the Allison Cook she'd evolved into in her own world. A sadist. A killer. Almost feral.

She bit into Wyatt's ear and felt blood in her mouth as her teeth pierced his flesh. The man screamed and started thrashing around with greater savagery, desperately slamming her against walls in an effort to dislodge her. She tore loose the piece of his ear and spat it away even as she drove a nail into one of his eyes. His screaming continued and turned shriller as he staggered out into the hallway with her still wrapped around him.

Allison was dimly aware of Jazz following them out of the room. She was yelling at them, but Allison was too lost in a haze of unthinking rage and hate to decipher her words. It was all just noise in those moments, no different from her own screaming and growling. She barely noticed as Wyatt tried slamming her into the hallway walls again and again. Her finger kept pushing deeper into his eye socket as they stumbled into the kitchen. She felt blood and ocular fluid ooze around her top knuckle. Her teeth were on his neck now, her mouth stretched wide across the flesh. She could feel the beating of his heart in the big vein beneath the layer of tender tissue.

The screen door in the kitchen flapped open and someone came in from the back stoop.

"What the hell?"

It was a southern-fried man's voice.

Hell came out sounding like *hail*.

Wyatt wailed in agony. "Get this crazy monkey bitch offa me!"

Allison's only response was another growl. She and Wyatt slammed up against the edge of the sink. Dirty plates fell away from one of the unwieldy stacks of dishes and shattered on the floor. Wyatt unleashed his shrillest scream yet as her teeth again began to puncture his flesh.

"Get the hell off my brother, bitch!"

Footsteps stomped toward her.

For a fraction of a second, Allison thought she might have to let go of Wyatt and deal with this new interloper, but two quick gunshots put an end to that. The other brother hit the floor with a heavy thud.

Blood filled Allison's mouth as she tore open Wyatt's throat. His knees buckled and he began to sag toward the floor. She unhooked her legs from behind him and kept her mouth pressed to his throat as she rode him all the way down. Her body shuddered in ecstasy as she swallowed the bloody piece of his flesh, the rumbling growl in her throat turning into a moan of pleasure.

Then, panting heavily, she pushed away from the dead man and sat on the floor with a satisfied grin on her blood-covered face. She turned her head and looked at Jazz, who was watching her with a stupefied expression. The gun was still in her hand, hanging loosely from her fingers now.

Allison laughed. "You should see the look on your face. I guess I disgust you now, huh?"

Jazz continued gaping at her in slack-jawed wonder a few moments longer. Then she began to smile. And laugh. "I'm sorry. I'm just sort of in shock. I didn't think you could ever get any hotter than you already were. Boy, was I wrong."

Allison got slowly to her feet.

THE UNSEEN II

She stepped over the outstretched legs of the man whose throat she'd just torn out and went to Jazz, drawing her into her arms. They stood right there in the midst of all the carnage and kissed for a long time.

Then they went back down the hallway to Jazlyn's bedroom.

THIRTY

THE NEXT MORNING ALLISON, STRETCHED out comfortably on Jazlyn's rumpled bed sheets, drifted in and out of sleep. Hazy fragments of pleasant dreams kept recurring, intermingling with fuzzy waking fantasies in those moments when consciousness briefly returned. Profoundly influenced by last night's sexual antics with Jazz, the dreams and fantasies were echoes of those revelatory experiences. Even in her drowsy state, she was aware of a deep contentment beyond anything she'd felt in a long, long time.

Reaching out for Jazz, her hand found only an empty section of mattress. She felt a small twinge of disappointment, but was still too sleep-fuzzy to let it bother her much. A slide back into the velvet comforts of dreamland was well underway when Jazz reentered the room and climbed atop her, straddling her midsection. Allison smiled and made a soft sound of pleasure.

A hard slap across the face snapped her eyes open.

A spike of adrenaline hit her system when she saw the girl's snarling expression of rage, rendering her instantly awake and alert. She gasped in fright when she saw the gun pointed at her face. Her mind was reeling in those first seconds, unable to comprehend anything about what was happening. She wanted to believe she was still asleep but having a nightmare now, her brain having taken a sharp and sudden turn into darker mental territory. That happened frequently when she made the mistake of going to bed sober, as she had last night.

Then she felt the muzzle of the gun press into the space between her eyes and knew for sure this was actually happening.

She just couldn't fathom why.

Not at first.

Jazz was breathing so hard through her clenched teeth she sounded like a runner near the end of a sprint. Her finger was inside the trigger guard of the gun, touching the trigger. One twitch could punch a hole through the middle of Allison's head, sending bits of her brain and skull into the pillow beneath her. She felt a deeper sense of nerve-twisting fear than she had at any point last night. The girl's expression of accusatory rage had a lot to do with that. It was a fury that burned deep in her soul, demanding violent release.

Allison opened her mouth to say something.

Jazz smacked her across the face with the butt of the gun. "You fucking cunt! I should kill you right fucking now!"

Allison spent another few moments mired in absolute confusion, the imminent threat of having her brains blown out still making it hard to think straight. The only thing she could latch onto was that this was a direct result of something she'd done. It wasn't just from out of nowhere.

Then she went still as a corpse.

Only one thing could have provoked a response of such extreme emotion from the girl who only hours ago was proclaiming her love for her and taking her to new heights of transcendent passion. Her conscience twinged at her again, offering more proof it wasn't completely dead yet.

Her eyes misted with tears. "I'm sorry, Jazz."

The girl sneered, bitterness radiating from her every pore. "Sorry's not good enough, you lying bitch. You used me. Led me on. You took advantage of my love for Allie Cook." Her bottom lip quivered as tears streamed from her eyes. "I felt so special for a little while last night, for maybe the first time in my worthless life. It was you who made me feel that way, but it was all a fucking hoax."

Allison grimaced. "You're still special. I'm sorry. I really am. I did what I did because I thought it was the only way to save my life."

An instinctive sigh of relief escaped her lips when Jazz tossed the gun aside. Her immediate assumption was that the girl's explosion of rage was burning itself out. That she was getting through to her, making her see the sense in what she was saying. She still wouldn't be happy about any of it, but the immediate moment of extreme danger was over.

This perception lasted only until Jazz curled her right hand into a fist and smashed it across Allison's jaw, eliciting a shrill cry of pain. The first blow was followed by a second and a third in rapid succession. These weren't half-hearted punches. They were delivered with force and savage intent. A fourth blow crashed against her mouth, loosening one of her teeth. Blood leaked from her gums. Allison could do nothing to fend the blows off because her arms were pinned beneath Jazz's legs. The girl was screaming at her, that hate blazing in her eyes again.

Then Jazz abruptly broke off the assault and climbed off her. She yelped as Jazz grabbed a handful of her hair and twisted it in her hand before hauling her off the bed. The pressure on her scalp was excruciating as the girl dragged her out of the room.

Out in the hallway, she tried getting to her feet, but Jazz was moving too fast. She was forced to blindly scramble forward on her hands and knees as the girl continued to pull her along. Her adversary was strong and more sturdily built than she was. She was taller, too, with a long stride. It wasn't long before Allison realized her ongoing desperate attempts to reason with her were doomed to fail, so she stopped trying. Her eyes darted everywhere as they passed through the living room, where the heel of her hand landed on a cockroach crawling through the filthy shag carpeting, squashing it. She was hoping to identify some means of fighting back against Jazz, some way of at least slowing her down.

She reached out and slapped a hand against the jamb as they passed through the archway into the kitchen. Her hand held fast to the jamb for a fleeting moment, the muscles in her arms straining hard against the force being exerted against her. She tried planting a foot on the floor to boost herself up, but the foot slipped out from under her as Jazz pulled at her hair even harder. She fell through the archway into the kitchen, landing hard on her back. Jazz dragged her across the blood-spattered linoleum floor, guiding her sliding form around her dead brothers as she headed for the screen door and the back stoop beyond.

Leading with her shoulder, Jazz bashed open the screen door and dragged Allison out onto the little stoop. Instead of then dragging her down the three steps to the ground, she heaved her into the yard. Allison landed in an awkward heap, one of her arms folding painfully beneath her. Raw survival instinct compelled a graceless attempt to get to her feet. She'd almost made it when a foot connected solidly with her ass and drove her back down to the ground. A fist drilled into the small of her back when she immediately made a second attempt to stand. This blow sent a briefly incapacitating lance of agony up the length of her spine, forcing her to drop to her hands and knees again.

She squealed as Jazz again grabbed a handful of her hair and started dragging her farther out into the yard. She laughed at Allison as she screamed and cried out for help. Of course she was laughing. There was no one around to hear her scream. No one was coming to her rescue.

The last time she was out in this yard was at night, but this was happening in bright early morning sunlight. If by some wild chance someone did come along about now, they'd be treated to the bizarre spectacle of two naked women locked in a fearsome physical struggle outdoors. She envisioned the scene as viewed through the lens of her camcorder, recording onto grainy old VHS tape. It was something she'd love if she saw it in some sleazy lost grindhouse classic of the 1970s, but existing in the midst of it in real life inspired other emotions, sheer terror being the main one.

As they passed near the big tree in the middle of the yard, she spotted the curled length of chain on the ground. "Oh, Jesus. Don't chain me up like some animal. Please, you've got to let me explain."

The girl laughed as she again threw Allison to the ground and punched her in the face when she made yet another attempt to stand. "Chaining you up is too good for you, bitch. That's for pets. You deserve something way worse. And I don't need to hear your fucking excuses."

She continued kicking and hitting Allison as she drove her toward the back of the yard. They were less than ten feet from the tree line when Jazz stepped on her back, pushing her face-first to the ground. She felt dirt in her mouth and lifted her head to spit it out as Jazz moved ahead of her and knelt on the ground. At first it wasn't obvious what she had in mind, but Allison started to have an inkling as the girl swept a thin layer of dirt off the lid of a pine box buried in the ground.

Jazz removed a padlock from a hasp and opened the creaky lid.

Allison trembled as she shook her head. "No . . . don't."

Jazz sneered as she got to her feet. "Bad girls go in the hole, bitch, and you're as bad as it gets. *This* is what you deserve, you fucking imposter. You fucking phony-ass cunt."

Allison tried rising up on her hands and knees again, but she had little strength remaining after this brutal thrashing. She was still having trouble moving without feeling like she had a hot poker rammed up her spine. Jazz grabbed hold of her, wrestled her over to the box, and dumped her inside it. The bottom of the box wasn't padded. The solid ground beneath it meant there wasn't much give when her back hit the wood. Landing on a slab of concrete wouldn't have been any less painful.

Standing at the edge of the rectangle of excavated soil, Jazz looked down at Allison and smiled. "Sweet dreams, bitch."

She flipped the lid shut with her foot.

Allison started sobbing.

Seconds later, the padlock clicked shut somewhere above her.

THIRTY-ONE

THUS BEGAN ANOTHER LONG STRETCH of time imprisoned in a dark space. Having it happen twice in under twenty-four hours meant it was officially a trend, one Allison vowed to put a permanent end to should she be lucky enough to regain her freedom a second time. This time, at least, she had her hands free, but the space she was confined to was much smaller. She started experiencing symptoms of claustrophobia within the first few minutes, including a shortness of breath that had more to do with fear than oxygen deprivation. It was too soon for that, but her fingers clawed at the underside of the lid in a desperate frenzy anyway, splinters embedding in the flesh beneath her nails.

She continued feeling like she was on the verge of suffocation until she spied the airholes drilled into the lid. There were just two of them, small circles of light right above her feet at the opposite end of the box. She chose to interpret their presence as an indication that confinement to "the hole" wasn't necessarily intended as a death sentence.

Also, the lid of the box being no more than an inch or two below ground level suggested banishment to it was mostly about punishment and behavior modification. Maybe at some point Jazz would decide she'd suffered enough and let her out. Allison wanted to believe such an outcome was possible, but she was also angry with herself for allowing the idea space in her head.

Maybe the dead matriarch of this white trash dumpster fire of a family had utilized The Hole primarily as a means of psychological torture, but it didn't necessarily follow that Jazz had the same purpose in mind. It was just as likely she'd leave Allison out here to starve to death over a period of days. Keeping this possibility at the forefront of her mind felt of utmost importance. She feared she might be jinxing herself by entertaining even the slightest glimmer of optimism. That was the kind of thinking she'd spent most of her life dismissing as superstitious bullshit, but things had changed. She knew now there was good reason to fear strange things that lurked in shadows and manipulated people and events, often for reasons obscure and impossible to understand.

She stopped clawing at the lid and willed herself to calm down. In a few minutes, the effort began to pay off, as her breathing evened out and her heart rate returned to a normal range. She stretched out as best she could, but the box clearly had not been constructed with comfort in mind. Not only was it not nearly long enough to accommodate a woman of average build, it was stiflingly narrow and had a depth of no more than two feet. She felt like she'd been crammed into a child's coffin. This did not stop her from trying to get at least moderately comfortable anyway, as she twisted and contorted herself around every possible way she could manage. None of it helped. If anything, her discomfort level worsened.

It occurred to her to wonder how a man of average physical stature could fit in here at all. Then it came to her that the box simply hadn't been built with men in mind. This was only speculation. She knew little about this deranged clan and their predatory ways, but she suspected she was on the right track. They preyed almost exclusively upon women. Any men who ran afoul of them were probably just marched into the woods, shot dead, and dumped in a hole deeper than this one.

Allison stopped struggling, finally accepting the impossibility of what she was attempting. She went still and focused again on her breathing, trying hard not to let panic take control again. After close to an hour in the box, her thoughts slowed down and her eyes closed. Sleep encroached, something she'd thought wouldn't be possible until much later in the day.

Dreams far less pleasant than the ones she'd luxuriated in so recently assailed her. A killer tracked her in the dark through a wilderness area. She screamed and ran endlessly through woods that seemed to go on forever, sometimes glancing back to see the villain gaining on her. The dreams kept shifting. Sometimes the killer was her beloved Jason Voorhees, resolutely stalking her with trademark machete in hand. Other times it was Jazz following her, naked and covered in blood, her long fingernails transformed into Freddy Krueger-esque finger-knives. Jazz smiled every time she looked back at her. She was scarier than Jason. A few other times the stalker was The Visitor, whose dark and blurry form blended in with the forest in a way that made him close to invisible. Allison kept falling as heavy rain pummeled the forest floor, sliding in the mud as she scrambled to get back to her feet and resume running. The last time she looked back, Jazz was right behind her, finger-knives raised and arcing through the air.

Allison awoke with a small gasp.

She squinted against bright sunlight, instinct telling her some fundamental change had occurred even before she grasped the nature of the change. Turning her head, she saw the lid of the box standing open. She heard birds chirping and caught a glimpse of tree branches swaying in the breeze high above her.

There was no sign of Jazz.

At first she had a hard time trusting what she was seeing, fearing it was merely a fragment of another nightmare, this one taunting her with an illusion of unexpected reprieve or even salvation. She stared up at the bright sky for several minutes, waiting to hear cruel laughter accompanied by the lid slamming shut again. The lid, however, remained open and upright, and she heard nothing other than a slight stiffening of the breeze and more chirping from the birds. Her physical discomfort felt too painful and real, the confines of the box too solid against her cramped body. A sharpening chill in the air made her shiver, an unsettling cold caress against her exposed, naked flesh. Also, there was none of the malleable, surreal quality she associated with dreams.

She became certain she was back in the waking world, but the open lid and its implied promise of freedom didn't mean she was in the clear yet. Her window of opportunity here might well be a narrow one, and a cruel trick on the part of her lover-turned-tormentor remained a distinct possibility. Jazz might be lurking somewhere on the other side of the upraised lid, waiting to hear her stir.

Waiting to pounce.

The prospect instilled fear, but there was an underlying anger as well, a feeling that grew stronger as her mind replayed the events preceding her temporary entombment. She knew how it had happened, of course. The assault caught her off guard. Jazz had the advantage over her from the start and never allowed her so much as a second to get her bearings or attempt to fight back, a humiliating experience after feeling like such a fearsome and feral thing of nature last night. She couldn't allow it to happen again.

Wouldn't allow it to happen again.

She took one more moment to gather her strength. Then she began to uncoil herself from her contorted position and raised up high enough to peek over the edge of the lid. At first there was no sign of Jazz. She wasn't standing anywhere in the immediate vicinity of The Hole. Lifting her head higher, Allison did a more thorough visual sweep of the yard.

No sign of her anywhere. She looked at the back stoop. The screen door was closed, but the inner door was wide open, and she could see into the kitchen. Her gaze stayed on that view of the inside of the house for nearly a full minute, but she detected no signs of anyone moving around in there.

Then she lifted her head higher still, looked up, and there she was.

Jazz wasn't in the yard at all. Or in the house.

She was in the tree.

THIRTY-TWO

HER JOINTS STIFF FROM THE period of tight confinement, Allison groaned as she crawled out of the box and got shakily to her feet on solid ground. She moved away from The Hole and began a tentative approach toward the tree, glancing around for signs of anyone watching her. As far as she knew, there was no one left here to observe her, but she was incapable of feeling anything other than profoundly self-conscious about being unclothed outdoors.

The feeling faded as she moved around the tree and positioned herself for a better look at Jazz, who was hanging from the thick and sturdy branches of the big old oak. That she was dead was obvious from the moment Allison caught sight of her. All her limbs were broken in multiple places and twisted about in unnatural pretzel-like fashion. Her head was turned fully backward, the flesh of her neck twisted like taffy. Her fingers all looked like snapped twigs. No eyeballs remained in the bloody sockets.

Anyone else stumbling upon so grisly a sight would be screaming or running away by now, but Allison felt no fear. An enervating sense of morbid awe caused her to stagger backward a step before dropping to her ass on the ground. Feeling lightheaded, she decided to lie back, stretching out on the dead grass as she continued to marvel over the utter ruination of a once beautiful young girl. An angry part of her had desired revenge against Jazz for treating her so brutally. And yet now she also felt sadness.

The girl *had* saved her life, after all. She'd also opened up her world in a way, exposing her to new possibilities, things she would've gone on dismissing forever otherwise. Last night's explorations hadn't cured her of men, of course. She remained who she'd always been in that regard, but her horizons were definitely broader now.

She didn't spend much time trying to puzzle out how such a bizarre and gruesome fate had befallen the girl. Only one possible culprit existed. The Visitor did this while Allison was running from a form-shifting killer in her dreams. Then, when the deed was done, he freed her from The Hole. Hanging the dead girl's twisted and broken body in this manner was, at root, a macabre form of gift presentation.

Here is the one who hurt you, he was telling her. *I am your savior once again.*

As soon as she had this thought, she felt his presence in her head again, stronger now than at any other point since her arrival in this world. As always, there were no words, just knowledge slithering into her head like thought worms. He confirmed her suspicions. She was right about all of it.

Then he showed her other things.

A possible sustainable way forward in this new world. She smiled as she began to see the shape of it, how it would work, and how, if everything went just right, she could become happier than she'd ever been.

She got up and went into the house.

The bodies of the dead brothers were beginning to stink. She looked at the gaping, ragged hole in the neck of the one she'd killed and felt a warm rush of reflective satisfaction. A person who could do a thing like that could do *anything* with enough determination and perhaps a little assistance from a powerful ally.

She went back to Jazz's room and started rummaging through her things, turning up a stack of horror magazines in the closet. Sorting through them, she found the issue of *Rue Morgue* the girl mentioned last night, the one with an in-depth interview and profile of Allie Cook. She stretched out on the bed of her dead lover and read the magazine piece from start to finish, learning many illuminating things about her doppelganger.

A second thorough read-through of the article was followed by a resumption of her search of the room. She meticulously searched every square inch of the crowded closet, checked every drawer of the dresser, and even looked under the bed. The search turned up little of interest. Aside from her Blu-ray player and TV, the girl appeared to have owned no electronic devices. No phone, no iPad, no laptop, nothing. This made sense in context with some of the things she'd said last night. Jazz had existed as a slave in her own home, her pussy a money-making machine for her twisted family, thus it was likely they'd allowed her only minimal contact with the outside world. She was obviously allowed to use the internet on occasion for buying things like the signed Allie Cook poster, but probably only under strict supervision.

Allison went back out to the kitchen and took a phone off one of the brothers, the one Jazz shot dead. The phone was a newer model with facial recognition. She held the screen in front of his face to unlock it, returned to Jazz's bedroom, and spent some more time looking up every scrap of information she could find on Allie Cook.

When she was satisfied she'd learned all she could, she searched the house until she found the dead mother's room. On a little desk in a corner of the room was an ancient desktop computer, undoubtedly the one Jazz was allowed to sometimes use, probably with her mother looming over her the whole time, but Allison didn't care about that by then. She needed clothes, and she and the mother were comparable in size. She managed to put together a few acceptable outfits. None of the woman's clothes were of a style that appealed to her, but they were functional and that was all that mattered for now.

She found an old-fashioned hard-shell suitcase under the woman's bed. The clothes went in the suitcase, as did the issue of *Rue Morgue* and Jazz's collection of Allie Cook movies. A further examination of the girl's movie collection turned up an old DVD of *Friday the 13th Part IX: Homecoming*. That also got tucked away inside the suitcase. She still lamented the loss of the special edition Blu-ray the poor dead foot fetishist had purchased for her at Walmart, but the DVD would do for now.

In searching the rest of the house, she found a decent amount of cash stashed away in various places, more than enough to get her where she was going with probably plenty left over. She assumed it was all ill-gotten gains of the sort one wouldn't bother reporting to the government.

Out front of the house she found a recent model Toyota 4Runner, black with tinted windows. It was the perfect vehicle for her upcoming long journey out west. She assumed it belonged to one of the brothers. Well, he wouldn't be needing it anymore. The Visitor would not magically transport her across the country. He was saving his favors for a bigger task. She needed time to heal from the beating she'd taken anyway.

Allison stashed the suitcase in the 4Runner, along with all the beer from the fridge, stowed in an old Styrofoam cooler.

It wasn't even noon yet by the time she got out on the road.

THIRTY-THREE

Nine days later

THE LONG DRIVE OUT TO California was not without stumbling blocks. Most of the hiccups were things she anticipated based on her early experiences in this new world. Early on she had a harrowing encounter with relentless obsessive types at a gas station. A man in a silver Nissan Rogue followed her for miles until she pulled over to the side of a desolate road, where they got out of their vehicles and approached each other. He was smiling. She wasn't. He reached for her. She rammed the blade of a hunting knife into his throat, yanked it out, and walked away, leaving him bleeding and gasping on the side of the road.

At the next gas station, she purchased three hundred dollars' worth of prepaid Visa cards, enough junk food to last her a while, and the most expensive burner phone available. The cards allowed her to pay for gas without having to go into every store along the way, further reducing the necessity of being around other people. She downloaded all the popular social media apps to the burner phone and used them to stay updated on Allie Cook's activities. The filmmaker posted things with great frequency, which was helpful.

On the day Allison arrived to stake out the motel where she was staying, the director was a week away from wrapping principal photography on her latest movie, *The Killing Kind 2*, yet another one she was also appearing in as a performer. They were shooting in a small desert town far from her home in Los Angeles. The motel was isolated. The only neighboring buildings were a gas station on the other side of the two-lane desert highway and an out-of-business tiki bar.

She parked in the otherwise empty lot of the tiki bar that afternoon and watched as the cleaning lady methodically made her way down the sidewalk outside the line of motel rooms. Allison already knew her doppelganger was registered at the motel in room 109, information gleaned from a phone conversation with the not very bright clerk on duty. When the cleaning lady unlocked the door to 109 and went inside, Allison got out of the 4Runner and hoofed it over to the motel.

She walked fast, wearing sunglasses and a dark blue hoodie with the hood pulled down over the top portion of her face. Not the most inconspicuous attire for a desert locale, but she hoped it would stop potential obsessives from fixating on her. That was something she wouldn't have to worry about much longer if things went as planned, but for now it remained a necessary precaution.

Peeking in through the open door, she heard the heavyset woman working in the bathroom. She felt jittery as she stood there on the precipice of actually attempting this crazy thing, but she'd come too far and been through too much to let that stop her. Moving as quietly as she could, she slipped into the room and slithered her way under the bed.

She kept her breathing low and even as she listened to the woman come out of the bathroom and do the rest of her work, which included changing the sheets on the bed. Her thoughts during those tense moments almost entirely consisted of her deep wish for the woman to hurry up and leave. This desire did not come to fruition. The woman worked slowly, plodding around the room as she dusted all the faux-wood furniture and the blinds. She tended to other tasks as well, ones that weren't as easy to identify by sound alone.

Then, after a period that felt like it encompassed lifetimes, the woman walked out of the room, locking the door behind her. Allison crawled out from under the bed, availed herself of the newly clean bathroom, and sat down at the table next to the window. She opened the blinds just enough for her to see anyone approaching the room. Viewed from outside, they should still appear closed, especially if only given a cursory glance. She set the hunting knife and the gun she'd taken from Jazlyn's house on the table.

And she waited.

THIRTY-FOUR

SHE WAS DOZING MANY HOURS later when she heard the key slide into the door lock. This was a quaint old school motel, a relic from a long bygone era with little in the way of modern trappings. Among other things, there were no key cards. Only old-fashioned metal keys unlocked these doors.

Allison's eyes snapped open wide and she grabbed the gun right as the door began to creak open. There was just enough time to get the gun up and aimed. Allie Cook didn't see her sitting there until she'd already started to push the door shut.

Her hand froze on the door knob.

They locked eyes with each other.

Allison read multiple things in her doppelganger's shocked expression right away. There was surprise and fear, natural things for anyone to feel upon entering a room they expected to find unoccupied only to find a stranger inside waiting for them. Then came the immediate transition from instinctual fear to outright terror when the presence of the gun registered. And right after all that came that first spark of recognition, followed quickly by confusion and denial.

"Who the fuck are you?"

Allison smiled. "You know who I am. You just can't bring yourself to believe it. But before we're done here, you will. Trust me on that."

Allie Cook's expression remained a study in dumbfounded

confusion a moment longer. Then she shook her head. "Pretty sure I don't have any long-lost twin sisters nobody ever told me about. What are you, some obsessed fan who had plastic surgery to look like me?" Snide laughter followed this remark. "You did, didn't you? Too bad you obviously take shit care of yourself, because otherwise the illusion would be perfect. You look like I did eight years ago, when I was still on the booze."

Allison's expression hardened as she waved the director away from the door with the gun. "Have a seat on the bed. We're gonna have a little talk."

"Is that thing even real?"

Allison rose from the chair and approached the director, placing the muzzle of the gun against her forehead. "Does it look real?"

The filmmaker's attempt at asserting dominance over her with bluster and derision came to an end in that moment. Fear crept back into her expression as she let go of the doorknob and went to the bed. The strap of a backpack was slung over her right shoulder. She allowed it to slide to the floor before taking a seat at the foot of the bed.

Allison closed and locked the door.

Then she turned her chair toward the bed and sat again, keeping the gun pointed at Allie. "Okay, so let's just get right to it. I look like you because I am you. Sort of."

Allie Cook shifted uneasily on the edge of the bed. "Sort of? The fuck does that mean? More delusion, I imagine."

Allison shook her head. "Actually, it isn't, and I'll be proving it soon. Are you familiar with multiverse theory?"

The director squinted at her in a way that communicated a deepening conviction that she was dealing with an unhinged individual, an insight that clearly made her uncomfortable. "I'm familiar with it, yes." She enunciated the words slowly, purposely dragging them out as she scrambled for a way to handle the crazy person that didn't end with her being shot. "Are you trying to say you're a version of me from an alternate reality?"

Allison nodded. "That's exactly what I'm saying, because it's the stone-cold fucking truth. In fact, it's likely there's an infinite number of alternate Allison Cooks spread across all the planes of existence. I'm probably one of the shittier versions, if you want to know the truth. I've never really accomplished much, unlike you. I had ambitions once upon a time, but I didn't have the confidence I needed to realize them. Also unlike you. You're everything I ever wanted to be but couldn't become because I was so fucked up."

A strange thing happened as the director listened to this. Instead of becoming infused with more skepticism and fearfulness, the look on her face turned sympathetic. "Look, I can hear the pain in your voice. I don't believe you're me from another world, but I do believe you're hurting, that you feel like you're at the end of your rope. You need help, and I can see to it that you get it."

Allison laughed. "How fucking altruistic of you. Very on-brand for Allie fucking Cook." More bitter laughter. "You don't believe me? Okay, here's the proof I promised."

Thus began a long and intimately detailed recitation of secret personal things only a teenage Allison Cook would know. Things she never would have shared with anyone, regardless of how close the relationship.

Allie Cook's eyes widened as she listened.

She sat trembling on the edge of the bed. "How do you know any of that? I planned to take that shit about Dad to my grave. Never breathed a word of it to *anyone*."

Allison nodded. "Neither did I."

The director's eyes filled with tears. "It's true, isn't it? All of it. You're really another version of me."

Allison didn't reply to that.

She didn't need to now.

The director wiped her eyes. "I don't understand. How is this possible? What do you even want with me?"

Allison smiled. "Wow. A lot to unpack with all that. I'll keep it as simple as I can. I recently became bonded with a strange creature who can travel between realities. How that happened is a long story. We won't bother with that. But the creature is what I guess you'd call a kind of psychic vampire. He preys on my emotions and desires. Feeds on them. It's changed me, made me less human. Before leaving my world, I did some bad things. Crazy things. I was backed into a corner. Things looked bleak. Things didn't seem much better when I got here. There was a . . . well, let's just call it a complication. One I didn't think I'd be able to get past until The Visitor showed me a way out."

Allie Cook frowned. "The Visitor? That's the vampire thing you were talking about?"

"Yep."

The director glanced at the door.

She was probably itching to make a run for it.

Allison hoped that wouldn't happen, because she'd be forced to intervene. A violent struggle could result in an outcome detrimental to what she was here to accomplish. So she got up and put herself in front of the door.

"You're not going anywhere, so just get that idea out of your head." She pointed the gun at the filmmaker again. "You even try it, I'll blow your fucking brains out."

She had no intention of doing any such thing, but Allie Cook didn't need to know that.

Allie sighed. "Fine. What's this way out you mentioned? Does it involve killing me? It does, doesn't it? Why else would you have that fucking gun?"

Allison shook her head. "I'm not here to kill you. I don't want to hurt you at all, in fact. That complication I mentioned? Turns out there's a way to negate it and live a peaceful, normal life here. It's a matter of restoring balance between the worlds."

Allie Cook looked confused again. "What the hell are you talking about?"

Allison moved away from the door, keeping the gun leveled at the filmmaker's midsection as she approached the bed. "Come on, Allie, you're smarter than this. I know you can see it. Sense it. You're just in denial. Feeling desperate. We're gonna swap places. You'll go to my world and take my place there and I'll stay here, taking over your life."

The director gaped at her silently for a moment.

Then she snorted derisive laughter. "That's insane. You can't just step into my life. You said it yourself, you didn't have the confidence to become what I am. What's more, you don't have my experiences. I've spent the last decade of my life making movies at a really high level. Do you really think you can just fake having that knowledge and ability?"

Allison shrugged. "I honestly don't know, but I'm gonna give it a shot. What's that thing you clean and sober types say in your little meetings? Oh, yeah. 'Fake it until you make it.' Sounds like a good strategy to me."

She moved another couple steps closer to the director.

Allie scooted backward some. "What are you doing? Stay away from me."

Allison laughed. "Not an option. We have to be in physical

contact at your moment of transference."

"Fuck that."

Allie leapt up off the edge of the bed and almost slipped around Allison by faking in one direction before ultimately going the other way. Allison dropped the gun as she wheeled around and caught Allie from behind, wrapping her up in a hug as she wrestled her back over to the bed.

The director screamed.

Allison clamped a hand over her doppelganger's mouth and stamped on her foot, hobbling her long enough to heave her onto the bed and climb atop her. The director squirmed beneath her, struggling with all her might to get free, but she was pinned to the mattress. Trapped.

Another scream.

And then she was gone.

Allison collapsed into the mattress with a sigh that was only a little sad.

THIRTY-FIVE

THE NEXT MORNING A CALL from someone named Theresa Wickman came in on Allie Cook's phone. Allison's immediate assumption was that Theresa was someone involved with her doppelganger's current film project. Only it wasn't her project any longer, was it?

Allison found the phone the previous evening while rifling through the contents of the director's backpack. Before turning in for the night, she spent some time scrolling through the woman's emails and contacts. This represented a new stage in the process of getting to know her better and preparing to take over her life. Her inbox was overflowing with messages from people unfamiliar to Allison. Some were personal in nature, but many were related to a dizzyingly wide range of business matters related to her filmmaking endeavors. She read the longer, more detailed ones thoroughly, familiarizing herself with the jargon used. At some point she'd have to start having real conversations with these people. Becoming fluent in the way they talked was a top priority. She would stumble at times, but believed she could bluff her way through the miscues.

Also helpful in this regard were Allie's text messages with numerous people, which included several from individuals with recognizably famous names. Popular culture in this world diverged from popular culture in the world she'd called home until recently, but there was a significant amount of overlap as well. The text threads with celebrities were fun to read, but the one that interested her the most was the longest of them all, consisting of several years of saved messages. She read it all the way back to the beginning, learning much that would be important in her new personal life.

Her caller that next morning left a nearly two-minute voicemail.

Allison listened to it and gathered that certain people were upset with her. Her on-set arrival was scheduled for hours ago and the delay was costing the production money it couldn't afford to squander. The caller was a young woman. Some kind of production assistant, it seemed. She spoke in a tone imbued with equal parts irritation and fearfulness. The poor girl was probably terrified of upsetting the famous director while feeling pressure from lots of other directions. Next Allison checked text messages sent to the phone while she was asleep. There were many, including one in SCREAMING ALL CAPS sent from someone she guessed was a pissed-off producer. Most were from people she didn't know yet, with one exception.

She sent a reply to that person.

Then she took a deep breath and called Theresa.

The call was answered right away. "Where the fuck are you? People are freaking out."

Allison cleared her throat. "Yeah, sorry. I had kind of a bad night. Food poisoning or something. And, uh, now my car's acting up. Could somebody come pick me up?"

Theresa sighed dramatically. "Jesus, Allie. You should've texted me as soon as you started feeling bad."

"I know. I'm fucking sorry, okay?"

Another big, dramatic sigh. "It's fine, whatever. I'll come get you. Be ready to roll in twenty minutes."

The line went dead.

Allison changed out of the drab outfit she'd been wearing for the last few days and into some of the director's clothes. She looked and felt better as soon as the transition was complete. More like the Allie people here knew. She zipped up the backpack, slung it over a shoulder, grabbed the keys and phone that now belonged to her, and went outside to wait for Theresa.

The girl was a svelte stunner in a miniskirt and retro white go-go boots. She looked like a time traveler from the swinging 1960s. She was also hyper as hell and babbled nonstop. Allison was fine with that. It delayed the necessity of having to fake technical filmmaking knowledge.

Once she arrived at the shooting location, she was assailed by a constant parade of people in apparent dire need of a moment of her time. She listened closely to what was said. One big thing that helped was that most of them already seemed perfectly aware of what needed doing and their role in making it all happen. She nodded a lot and frequently said things like, "Sounds good," and, "Yeah, let's do that." Other times she made sounds of clueless contemplation and deflected to others when she felt stuck. More often than not, those others were more than willing to offer their opinions on what to do, and in most cases Allison was able to make them happy by simply agreeing with them.

Actual movie stuff started happening.

A scene was set up. Actors took their places.

Allison got jittery.

A lot of expectant eyes turned in her direction. She thought about all the movies about making movies she'd seen. Many of them included scenes depicting moments just like this, minus the stand-in fake director aspect. She decided to proceed as if she were acting out one of those scenes. There was some predictable confusion at the start, but she managed to get things started. More confusion ensued, but Allison continued bluffing her way through it. A few people got frustrated with her, but no one accused her of being a fraud. The scene was set up again and additional takes were filmed. As the day progressed, she began to feel moderately more at ease.

The hilarious thing about all of it, from Allison's point of view, was that she still had no idea what the movie was even about.

At long last, the working day came to an end and Theresa drove her back out to the motel. She thanked the girl for the ride and, after solemnly promising her there'd be no repeat of this morning's debacle, she went into her room and devoted some more time to reading Allie Cook's personal messages.

Less than half an hour after her return to the motel, someone knocked on her door. She got up and looked through the peephole, smiling when she saw who it was.

She opened the door and let Cassie into the room.

Clad in a black dress with white polka dots, Allie Cook's wife strutted in on Louboutin heels. This version of Cassie was even more impressive than the one who'd been her best friend for years. There were many similarities. Same dyed-black hair with perfect bangs. Stunning fashion sense. But there was something different in the way she carried herself, a greater level of self-assurance and poise.

She handed Allison a bouquet of flowers and said, "Surprise!"

There were things she might have said at that point—or attempted to say—but then the woman was kissing her.

Words became unimportant for a while.

Later, as they were lying in bed entwined in each other, Allison said, "I came up with a concept for a new movie. Kind of a found footage thing. I think it could be pretty cool. Want to hear it?"

Cassie interlaced fingers with her and smiled. "Thrill me."

Allison laughed. "Ooh, Tom Atkins reference. No wonder I fell in love with you. Anyway, I had this image in my head. A young woman living alone somewhere in the Midwest. She's got one of those old camcorders and she sort of uses it to document her own descent into madness and murder. This happens in the dead of snowy winter. She goes outside inappropriately attired a lot because she's losing it so badly. At first you think it's just an exercise in psychological horror, but it turns out she's being manipulated by a strange creature. A psychic vampire kind of thing you only ever see as a shadowy blur. I was thinking of calling it *The Unseen Things*. What do you think?"

Cassie's expression was thoughtful.

She began to nod. "Yeah. I can totally see it in my head. I think it could be pretty great. Maybe we could start working out a full treatment once you're done with this current thing, but maybe not rush into it full-bore right away."

Allison frowned. "Why not?

Cassie smiled and snuggled closer. "Because a little birdie told me that new *Friday the 13th* reboot might finally be moving ahead at Paramount. And word has it you're at the top of their list to direct. I'm assuming you'll be able to whip up a wow-level pitch for them."

Allison gaped at her a moment before saying, "Holy fucking shit." She sat up and put her back against the headboard. "Oh my fucking God."

Cassie laughed. "That priceless fucking look on your face is exactly why I came out to see you in person rather than telling you over the phone. This is your dream, babe. What you've always wanted."

Allison slowly shook her head, still reeling from astonishment. "You know what? This just might be the happiest moment of my entire fucking life. I never believed anything this amazing could happen to me."

"Nobody deserves it more than you. Nobody on this fucking planet."

Allison smiled. "Fuck it. You're right. I deserve this. I deserve everything."

"Damn right."

Sensing something, Allison glanced at the opposite side of the room and caught a glimpse of The Visitor standing by the door. He wore his usual long black coat and black hat pulled down low over his blurry face. She tensed, feeling her arms prickle with gooseflesh even though she knew she had nothing to fear. This was no random materialization.

It was a reminder.

He would always be with her.

Always be watching.

She looked right at his partially hidden face and nodded. *I'll never reject you. I'll always let you have what you need from me. The darkness inside is still with me and always will be.* After that, he faded from view like a dispersing mist.

Cassie frowned and craned her head around to look at the door. "What are you looking at?"

Allison slid away from the headboard and wrapped herself around the woman, lightly biting her on the shoulder. "Yum." She laughed. "You taste good. Maybe we should think about getting into cannibalism."

Cassie clasped hands with her. "We totally should."

She laughed.

Allison nipped her shoulder and laughed again, too, even though she wasn't joking, which was something Cassie didn't need to know.

Not yet.

~

The new patient was losing her damn mind again. Elton MacKinnon got up from his desk with a groan and went down the hallway to check on her for what felt like the hundredth time that night. She was only two days into her indefinite confinement to the state-run mental hospital, but already she struck Elton as a hopeless case.

He peeked in at her through the slot in the door. "You need to settle down in there, Miss Cook. I know you don't want to hear it, but you're not getting out of here any time soon. The acting out won't help you one bit."

The patient was wearing a restraint safety jacket for her own protection. She was deemed a suicide risk earlier in the week after repeatedly slamming herself against the bars of her jail cell. Then came a hearing which resulted in her transfer to the hospital. A stay at the facility might reduce her risk of self-harm in the short term, but her prospects beyond that appeared grim.

She was a killer.

A bloody-thirsty butcher and cannibal.

A shiver still went up Elton's spine every time he heard the grisly details. The chopped-up body of the mystery woman found in Allison Cook's house. The carefully wrapped packages of human meat discovered in her refrigerator. The severed head stashed in her freezer. He'd read the official reports and knew a little more than what made it to the media reports. The stuff that made the news was lurid and stomach-churning enough without some of those extra details. Like the chilling transcripts of deranged ramblings she'd for some reason felt compelled to commit to videotape, evidence so damning and irrefutable she'd never stand a chance in court. Or the stuff about the basement. The bucket of organs. The dog cage and the shit-and-piss-stained blankets.

The woman he was looking at through the slot was a monster.

She was standing in the middle of her room with her back facing him, but now she turned toward him and smiled, her scraggly, dirty hair hanging in her face. "Hi, Elton."

The orderly sighed.

It was the same routine every time.

Fake friendliness followed by . . . well, insanity.

"You need to chill, Miss Cook. If you can't, I'm authorized to dope you to the gills. Is that what you want?"

Still smiling, the woman approached the door and leaned close to the slot to speak. "You need to listen to me. Like, *really* listen. No one is really hearing what I'm telling them and I'm starting to lose my fucking mind over it."

Elton grunted.

No shit.

"I'm not the Allison Cook who killed those people. I'm not a crazy murderer. I'm really fucking not." She started to cry as she continued. "I'm from another reality where I'm a famous movie director. Allison Cook the killer is there right now. She took my place and sent me here. Please, you've got to help me fix this. You've got to help me get back home."

She began to weep uncontrollably, hanging her head despondently.

Elton allowed some silent moments to tick by.

Then he said, "All due respect, Miss Cook, none of that's true. None of that's even possible. The sooner you accept that, the better off you'll be."

The woman lifted her head and shook the greasy hair out of her eyes. "All due respect, Elton, but you're a simple-minded orderly, not a fucking doctor."

Elton sighed.

And here came the insults again. Like clockwork. Every. Fucking. Time. A million fucking times, seemingly, in just two goddamn days. He wasn't sure how much more he could take. Perhaps it was finally time to consider a career change.

"I'm sorry you feel that way, Miss Cook. Now unless there's something else—"

She launched herself at the door, pushing her open mouth into the slot and gnashing her teeth at him.

"*Let me out! Let me out! Let me out!*"

He flinched away from the door, his back meeting the opposite wall a second later. His heart pounded painfully hard in his chest as he listened to her growl like an animal and repeatedly slam herself against the door.

Okay, then, he thought. *If that's the way you want it. Fine.*

He went off to unlock the dope locker and find someone to help him. This was definitely a job for at least two strong men. He was likely to wind up getting his nose bitten off if he tried dealing with that she-demon alone.

He shook his head as he hurried down the hallway.

That crazy bitch ain't ever getting out of the nuthouse.

Behind him, the she-demon howled like a wild creature of the night.

Bryan Smith is the author of numerous novels and novellas, including *68 Kill*, *The Unseen*, *Slowly We Rot*, *Depraved*, and *Kill For Satan!*, which won a Splatterpunk Award for best horror novella of 2018. He won a second Splatterpunk Award in 2020 for *Dirty Rotten Hippies and Other Stories*. He is also the co-author of *Suburban Gothic*, written with Brian Keene. *Last of the Ravagers*, a splatter western, is forthcoming from Death's Head Press. A film version of *68 Kill*, directed by Trent Haaga and starring Matthew Gray Gubler from *Criminal Minds*, was released in 2017. He lives in Tennessee with his dog Mac.

Other Grindhouse Press Titles

#666__*Satanic Summer* by Andersen Prunty
#084__*Waif* by Samantha Kolesnik
#083__*Racing with the Devil* by Bryan Smith
#082__*Bodies Wrapped in Plastic and Other Items of Interest* by Andersen Prunty
#081__*The Next Time You See Me I'll Probably Be Dead* by C.V. Hunt
#080__*The Unseen* by Bryan Smith
#079__*The Late Night Horror Show* by Bryan Smith
#078__*Birth of a Monster* by A.S. Coomer
#077__*Invitation to Death* by Bryan Smith
#076__*Paradise Club* by Tim Meyer
#075__*Mage of the Hellmouth* by John Wayne Comunale
#074__*The Rotting Within* by Matt Kurtz
#073__*Go Down Hard* by Ali Seay
#072__*Girl of Prey* by Pete Risley
#071__*Gone to See the River Man* by Kristopher Triana
#070__*Horrorama* edited by C.V. Hunt
#069__*Depraved 4* by Bryan Smith
#068__*Worst Laid Plans: An Anthology of Vacation Horror* edited by Samantha Kolesnik
#067__*Deathtripping: Collected Horror Stories* by Andersen Prunty
#066__*Depraved* by Bryan Smith
#065__*Crazytimes* by Scott Cole
#064__*Blood Relations* by Kristopher Triana
#063__*The Perfectly Fine House* by Stephen Kozeniewski and Wile E. Young
#062__*Savage Mountain* by John Quick
#061__*Cocksucker* by Lucas Milliron
#060__*Luciferin* by J. Peter W.
#059__*The Fucking Zombie Apocalypse* by Bryan Smith
#058__*True Crime* by Samantha Kolesnik
#057__*The Cycle* by John Wayne Comunale
#056__*A Voice So Soft* by Patrick Lacey
#055__*Merciless* by Bryan Smith
#054__*The Long Shadows of October* by Kristopher Triana
#053__*House of Blood* by Bryan Smith
#052__*The Freakshow* by Bryan Smith